7/24/15

LAFOURCHE PARISH PUBLIC LIBRARY

0 0533 0074 4159 5

Y0-AQT-828

R

Praise for Karen Stivali's
Leave the Lights On

"It simply is a perfect story; charming characters, a believable plot, sexy fun, and flawless writing have sold me on author Karen Stivali."

~ *Guilty Pleasures Book Reviews*

"The perfect contemporary romance. An entertaining, well-written book with an authentic love story that took complete hold of my mind, body and soul from the very first page."

~ *Harlequin Junkie*

"Very well written and very steamy!"

~ *Love Romance Books*

"The emotions are so real, the characters perfectly flawed...*Leave The Lights On* is another to add to the collection of stories I've enjoyed by Ms. Stivali."

~ *Storm Goddess Book Reviews*

"An absolute *gem* of a story and one that I can recommend without hesitation!"

~ *Swept Away By Romance*

Look for these titles by
Karen Stivali

Now Available:

Then, Again
Four Days to Forever

Leave the Lights On

Karen Stivali

SAMHAIN
PUBLISHING

Lafourche Parish Library

Samhain Publishing, Ltd.
11821 Mason Montgomery Road, 4B
Cincinnati, OH 45249
www.samhainpublishing.com

Leave the Lights On
Copyright © 2013 by Karen Stivali
Print ISBN: 978-1-61922-203-8
Digital ISBN: 978-1-61921-558-0

Editing by Christa Soule
Cover by Angela Waters

This book is a work of fiction. The names, characters, places, and incidents are products of the writer's imagination or have been used fictitiously and are not to be construed as real. Any resemblance to persons, living or dead, actual events, locale or organizations is entirely coincidental.

All Rights Are Reserved. No part of this book may be used or reproduced in any manner whatsoever without written permission, except in the case of brief quotations embodied in critical articles and reviews.

First Samhain Publishing, Ltd. electronic publication: November 2013
First Samhain Publishing, Ltd. print publication: November 2014

Dedication

My eternal gratitude to Nikka Michaels, my tireless beta reader, for loving Parker and for always being there for me.

Many thanks to Tiffany Reisz for her invaluable insight and her superhero-like speed-reading ability.

This book is dedicated to Mandy Pennington because I wish her nothing but happily ever afters and because she brightens my day, every day.

I can't imagine not having the three of you in my life.

Chapter One

Parker Wood pulled into the circular drive of the house he'd grown up in, as he'd done a thousand times, but it didn't feel like coming home. It felt like starting over. He couldn't help but notice the immaculate condition of the lawn. Every shrub, every tree, every mulch bed, groomed to absolute perfection even though the house had sat empty for over three months. A perk of owning the most successful landscaping-design company in the area.

The door of his Land Rover creaked as he opened it, the only flaw he'd found with the vehicle since he'd driven it off the lot two days earlier. He stepped onto the cobblestone drive, careful to make sure his feet landed on level surfaces. He'd never imagined that twenty-four could feel like eighty-four, but today it did.

"You can't expect to spend two days on your feet and not have it take a toll on you," his physical therapist Tanya had said to him as she dug her hand into the sorest spot on his hip.

"I expect to be able to do a hell of lot more than that." Parker had gritted his teeth and tried not to cringe as she pushed harder. Sparks of pain shot down his leg, but he knew that was good. With the number of surgeries he'd had after the accident, he knew he was lucky to have any sensation in his leg. Pain was a reminder that he could still feel.

"Patience, my dear. Not your strong suit, I know. Think about how far you've come this year. When I first met you, you could hardly stand. Now I can barely keep up with you when you walk. You're strong as an ox, Parker. This leg is ninety percent healed. You just overdid it. And the stress doesn't help."

Pain he could handle, but the comment made him flinch. He closed his eyes as she continued to work her fingers into him, pressing every excruciating spot she could find. None of it hurt more than the memory of the last two days. He'd hoped his first days out of the rehab center would be memorable in a good way, but instead he'd spent them at his father's wake and funeral. He breathed through his nose, trying to focus on the pungent scent of menthol rather than thinking about the fact that now that he was finally going home, his father wouldn't be there anymore. At only sixty, his body had lost its battle with prostate cancer. Parker couldn't help but wonder if the stress of having his only child in medical facilities for two years hadn't caused his father's condition to worsen.

Blowing out a long, slow breath, he hoisted a box out of the backseat. He made his way to the front door, amazed by how much everything looked the same. The brick front of the house, the ivy-covered trellis, the granite steps leading to the heavy black double doors. For a moment, he imagined it was three years earlier, and he was home from college for summer break—that the box he carried contained things he'd packed up from his dorm, that he'd find his father sitting at the kitchen table, reading a newspaper and muttering about the housing market.

He unlocked the door and stepped inside, holding his breath. The silence that greeted him knotted his stomach. *I'm home.*

The house smelled musty, but familiar. He set the box down at the base of the stairs. Hardwood floors. He never in his life thought he'd be so happy to see wood floors. Two years of the linoleum of hospitals and rehab made them a welcome sight. He ran his hand over the smooth curved banister. *Stairs. And I can actually climb them again.*

The knock at the door startled him. He whirled to see Mr. Nardo dressed in his mailman uniform, taking a tentative step into the house.

"Hey Mr. N."

"I figured it was your car in the driveway." Mr. Nardo's kindly eyes looked into his, full of sympathy. Parker could only hold the gaze for a second.

"Yeah, just got here. Unpacking the truck." He shoved his hands into his pockets, trying to strike a natural pose. The ache in his leg returned. *Stress makes it worse,* Tanya's voice echoed in his head.

"I was real sorry to hear about your dad."

Parker nodded. "Thanks."

"He'll be missed around town. Good man."

Parker studied the floor again, raising one hand to massage the back of his neck.

"You doing okay, kid? You need anything?"

"No, thanks. I'm good. Got the okay from the docs to start work on Monday."

Sympathy passed across Mr. Nardo's face again, followed by an encouraging smile. "I heard you were taking over the business. I bet your dad was real proud to know he was leaving everything in good hands."

"Yeah, I think he was." Parker felt desperate to change the subject. "How's Joey doing?"

Mr. Nardo's eyes lit up. "He's doing great. Still can't believe my boy's playing in the big leagues."

"You always knew he would."

The smile left Mr. Nardo's expression. "It shoulda been both of you, kid."

"Another lifetime." Parker shrugged.

Mr. Nardo nodded and clapped him on the shoulder. "They say things happen for a reason."

"That's what my dad told me the whole time I was in the hospital."

"Like I said, good man." He patted Parker's arm before stepping back out onto the porch. "It's good to see you, kid."

"You too, Mr. N." Parker leaned against the doorframe as Mr. Nardo descended the stairs. He turned around as he started across the walkway. "You know you're not the only kid back in town. Sophie Vaughn just moved back into her parents' place."

Parker's gaze automatically shot to the next yard, to Sophie's house.

Mr. N chuckled. "I thought that might get your attention."

Parker's cheeks prickled with heat. He and Joey had taken turns having a crush on Sophie since grade school, but neither of them had ever dated her. "I thought she got married."

"She did. And divorced. Her parents moved down to Florida full-time a few months back, so she decided to move into their place. Just moved in a few weeks ago. You should go say hi."

Parker's heart pulsed an extra beat. "I may just have to do that. Thanks for the heads-up."

"Any time, kid." Mr. Nardo continued down the path, climbed into the mail truck and drove down the street.

Sophie Vaughn tried to control the nervous fluttering in her stomach as she peered out her kitchen window for what seemed like the hundredth time in an hour. She swiped a finger full of chocolate frosting from the bowl on the counter and glanced at the Rubbermaid cake holder, hoping she'd put enough frosting on the actual cake. *Maybe I should pipe some around the bottom edge.* Her thoughts were interrupted by the sound of a car door slamming. She glanced out the window just in time to see Parker heading up his walkway, arms full of groceries.

He's home. Her heart doubled its rhythm. She'd barely been able to believe her eyes when she'd seen him the day before. The possibility of him moving back to his dad's house had crossed her mind when she'd heard that he was taking over the landscaping company. Seeing him unloading boxes out of the truck had made it a reality. They were neighbors again, after all these years.

Sophie gave her finger a final lick then washed her hands. *You can do this.* She inhaled deeply. *You're just paying condolences to an old friend. Nothing wrong with that.*

Except that she knew that wasn't all she was doing. This wasn't any old neighbor or any old friend. This was Parker Wood. The boy she'd spent years palling around with, hoping against hope that one day he'd see her as more than just a buddy.

She shook off the thoughts before she got herself too freaked out and lost her nerve. *Do it.*

The walk across their yards seemed eternal. Standing at his front door with the cake holder balanced on her right hand, she reached for the doorbell. The chime echoed through the closed door, and Sophie wondered if she'd be able to stay upright until he answered. *Maybe this wasn't such a good idea. Maybe he's in the shower or...*

The sound of the latch clicking open made her mind go blank, and then there he was. Taller than the last time she'd stood so close to him, at least six foot two now. Jaw line even more chiseled. Hair a deeper shade of brown and longer than she'd ever seen it—long enough to give him a sexy just-out-of-bed look but not long enough to cover his still-breathtaking blue eyes. She'd spent years looking at guys' eyes and had never found another pair that compared to Parker's. Black-ringed irises so entrancing she felt like she could stare into

13

them forever. His expression remained emotionless until he made eye contact with her, and in a heartbeat, his entire face changed.

"Sophie," he said, surprise evident in his voice as a smile tugged at his gorgeous lips.

"At your service," she said. *What? Oh, God...*

He let out a laugh, giving her a quick look up and down. "Wow, you look so... You look great."

"So do you." She felt her cheeks flush from the compliment and the admission. "I heard about your dad. I'm really sorry."

"Thanks." Parker nodded and looked at the ground.

"I made you a cake." She held the container up. "I know a casserole or something is probably more traditional and practical, but when I need cheering up, I always want cake."

Parker eyed the container. "You made it?"

Sophie nodded. "It's my mom's old recipe."

"Chocolate fudge?"

"Yep."

"I still dream about this cake."

Sophie felt her eyes bug. *He said cake, not you.* "Good dreams, I hope."

His smile grew broader. "Sinfully good."

Something Sophie couldn't identify flickered through his eyes. A memory? She couldn't stop staring at him.

"Hey, you know I kind of make it a policy not to leave beautiful women with cake standing on my front porch. You wanna come in?"

Sophie nodded, not trusting her voice. Parker stepped aside, and she moved past him. *God, he smells good.* He closed the door and followed her into the kitchen. The house looked almost exactly like she remembered it. For a minute she felt as if she were back in high school, coming over to study for a test or watch a movie with him and Joey.

"I just got back from the grocery store, but I forgot to buy coffee. There's milk, though."

Sophie set the cake down on the kitchen table and watched as Parker got out plates. The muscles in his arm flexed as he reached up into the cupboard. A fading scar snaked around his biceps, disappearing under the sleeve of his black T-shirt. *Must be from the accident.* He turned and caught her staring, and she felt her cheeks heat again. Parker rummaged through a drawer and set down forks and a knife. Sophie removed the lid from the cake server and the scent of chocolate filled the air. She cut two slices, pleased to see the hungry look in Parker's eyes as she slid a plate toward him. "Hope it's as good as you remember."

"I'm not worried." He smiled as he took a forkful.

Sophie held her breath.

Parker's eyes closed as he chewed. "Oh, man, dreams don't do this justice."

A giggle escaped Sophie, and she couldn't keep from grinning. She scooped up a forkful. "Not bad. Even my mom might give this a thumbs up."

"How is your mom?" Parker was already halfway through his piece of cake.

"Good. She and my dad really like living in Florida full-time. They've got a big group of friends down there, so it's been perfect for them."

"So the house is yours now?"

Sophie shifted in her chair and twirled her fork through the frosting. "All mine. I can have parties whenever I want."

The deep, rich sound of Parker's laughter warmed Sophie to her core.

"God, I remember your parties."

"Me too." Sophie's stomach fluttered. What she remembered most was hoping that maybe at one of them Parker would see her as more than just the girl next door. But that had never happened.

"You want something to drink? I've got milk, orange juice or water." He stood up, and Sophie couldn't resist letting her eyes sweep over him again. So lean and muscular. More irresistible than ever.

"Milk would be great."

Parker opened the fridge, and Sophie laughed. Other than milk and orange juice, there appeared to be a six-pack of beer and a block of cheese. "I thought you said you just went to the grocery store."

"I did. I guess I need some practice in the food-shopping department."

"I'll say. Or maybe I should come back with a casserole."

"You can come back with or without a casserole."

Chapter Two

Parker stood at his doorway, watching as Sophie crossed the yard toward her house. The gentle sway of her hips kept him mesmerized. He didn't look away until she disappeared through her door. *Jesus, you idiot, you didn't make plans to see her again.* He hadn't even gotten her phone number. *Shit. Maybe at least her home number's the same.* It only took seconds for him to recall her parents' number. Even though he hadn't called it in ages, he'd dialed it nearly every day for years. It remained permanently engraved in his brain.

Saying that Sophie looked fantastic would be an understatement. He'd always thought she was cute, even in her glasses and pigtail days, and he'd certainly appreciated when she'd graduated into contact lenses and curves, but none of that could have prepared him for what a striking woman she'd become. She was still as petite as he remembered—close to a foot shorter than him, with delicate bone structure—but her body had completely reproportioned itself. Fuller breasts, slimmer waist, more rounded curve to her hips. Even in jeans he could tell her legs were killer. Her dark almond-shaped eyes still had the same mischievous twinkle. He could feel himself smiling just from thinking about them. And he couldn't help wondering what was behind her mysterious grin. Wondering if her auburn hair felt as soft as it looked. Wondering what it would be like to wrap his arms around her and kiss her.

Jesus, get a grip. This was Sophie after all. The same Sophie who'd snuck into his house dozens of times after his dad had gone to bed to watch TV or play cards or just hang out and talk. The same Sophie who'd never shown the slightest bit of interest in him in over a decade of friendship. But then again, his hopeless crush on Sophie had been interrupted during their last year of high school by the arrival of Chrissie Barnes.

Although Chrissie was the last thing Parker wanted to think about, he couldn't help but remember the first time he'd laid eyes on her.

"Who the hell is that?" Joey had asked as they both watched her, long blonde curls bouncing in time with her steps as she walked into the main office on the first day of their senior year.

They'd tried to loiter long enough to see where she was headed but had been sent off to class by a cranky hall monitor. Parker spent the whole day scanning the halls for her but didn't see her again until after school.

He was stretching for a cross-country run, and she jogged right past him, wearing short shorts that showed off her perfectly toned legs, her breasts gently shifting under her tank top. He'd nearly fallen over. She made her way toward the cheerleaders and began warming up like she was one of them rather than a new girl there for tryouts. Parker kept his eyes on her as he jogged around the track.

Joey came up alongside him, breathing hard. "Now that's a damn shame."

"What is?" Parker asked.

"Newbie. You just know she's gonna hook up with someone from the football team. No way they're gonna let a sweet piece of ass like that get away."

Parker frowned, knowing Joey was likely correct. Cheerleaders always dated the guys from the football and basketball teams. "She hasn't even made the squad yet."

"Are you kidding me? Look at her move."

Parker turned just in time to see her do a double cartwheel and land in a split.

"Football player, by the end of the week," Joey said.

Parker couldn't keep his eyes off her. "You never know."

"I've been telling you for years, we gotta petition for baseball cheerleaders. We're the best players on the team. Baseball cheerleaders would be all over us. You could use that kind of sure thing." Joey punched him in the arm and broke into a full sprint.

As luck would have it, it wasn't a football player who'd turned her head. Much to Joey's surprise, Parker was the guy who caught her eye.

Chrissie had been everything Parker had ever wanted in a girlfriend. Beautiful. Smart. Funny. Sweet. And the most amazing kisser he could imagine. He couldn't count how many hours they'd spent pressed up against her locker in the hall, sneaking beneath the bleachers on the field, trying to maneuver around the gearshift in his beat-up old car—the pull toward her magnetic in its strength.

They'd only been going out for a few months when he'd gathered up his nerve and told her he was in love with her. When she repeated the words back, it had made him happier than he'd ever been. They were the "it" couple. At every party, hand in hand. Voted best couple at the senior prom. Parker had their whole future worked out. He got a full athletic scholarship to college, and Chrissie got accepted to a nearby university. They saw each on weekends, and after graduation, when he'd signed with a team and was bringing in money, they'd get married.

"You suck, you know that?" Joey would say every weekend when he was heading out to frat parties. "Worst. Wingman. Ever. You're like an old married man."

"Like you would have turned her down?"

"Shit, no. Chrissie's fucking great. Except for her taste in guys."

"She had enough good sense to avoid you."

"Much to the delight of every other woman on the planet."

"You haven't been with *every* other woman."

"Yet. Working on it." And he was. An endless stream of women paraded in and out of their dorm.

Parker couldn't even imagine it. In his mind he might as well have already been married. Not that he didn't look at other women, but he knew he loved Chrissie and wasn't about to risk what he had with her for a night of fun.

"She'd never find out." Joey would tell him.

"Wouldn't matter. I'd know." Lying wasn't something Parker was good at and that wasn't a characteristic he was looking to change.

"You don't know what you're missing, buddy."

That part was true. Truer than Joey even knew. But Parker stayed loyal.

By the end of their junior year in college, he was getting anxious to get on with his life. Scouts were coming to all the big spring games, and he knew he'd caught the eye of several. He and Joey were on the short list for several recruiters, and it was just a matter of time. Everything he wanted was so close he could taste it.

He'd come back to his dorm after three weekends in a row of away games, anxious as hell to finally spend some time with Chrissie. Seeing her sitting on his bed, waiting for him, he'd been so happy to be in the same room with her again it had taken him a minute to notice the look on her face. He pulled her into a kiss, surprised when he realized her face was damp with tears.

"What's wrong?" he asked, wiping beneath her eyes.

More tears spilled out of her, and Parker felt a pit growing in his stomach.

"Sweetie, what is it? Talk to me."

Chrissie bit her lip, unable to look at him.

Parker's heart beat faster as he rubbed her hand.

"I'm so sorry. I never meant for it to happen." She looked up at him, her big blue eyes still streaming tears. He saw sorrow and pity and fear. Tension knotted its way through him.

"Meant for what to happen?" He held still, not sure he wanted to hear the answer.

She dropped her gaze and her voice became a mere whisper. "There's someone else."

The words hit him like a punch, knocking the air out of him, but he was sure he must have misunderstood.

"What do you mean?" he asked, his throat so tight he could barely swallow.

"I met him in class a few months ago. I didn't mean for it to be anything but a friendship, but you've been away so much and..." She bit her lip again and took a deep shuddering breath. "It just happened."

"What did?" *Maybe they just went out on a date. Maybe she means she made out with him once, I could live with...*

"Parker, I'm marrying him. I'm pregnant."

Although a million thoughts jumbled around in his brain, not one could find its way past his lips. All he could do was stare at her.

She looked the same as always. Blonde curls tumbling over her shoulders, satiny cheeks rosy and flushed, tiny hands resting innocently in her lap. Perfect as a porcelain doll. Then she looked at him again, eyes rimmed with red and filled with the now-nauseating mix of pity and sorrow.

"Pregnant?" The word sounded so foreign coming out of Parker's mouth that he wasn't sure he'd pronounced it right. "With his kid?"

"I'm sorry."

The tingling numbness of shock ebbed, replaced by the searing heat of anger. Parker backed away from her on the bed, not wanting to be close to her but unsure if he could stand. Acid that had been pooling in his stomach surged up his throat high enough that he could taste the bitterness.

"Sorry? You're sorry?" His hands clenched so tightly his arms ached.

"I am." She reached for him, her hand grazing his shoulder before he could pull away. Her touch, familiar for so long, felt foreign. An unpleasant reminder rather than a caress. "I didn't mean..."

"To fuck someone?"

Chrissie flinched as if he'd slapped her. "It wasn't like that..."

"So you didn't fuck him? This was an immaculate conception?"

"I mean, I just—"

Parker found the strength to stand and paced the length of the room, his hand raking through his hair as he tried to contain his thoughts. "And you're *marrying* him?" He stared at her, still not believing that her answer could possibly be yes.

She held his gaze for what seemed like an eternity. He watched in awe as she nodded. "I love him."

That did it. Every bit of self-control drained out of him, and all he felt was anger. "Get out." He strode to his door and held it open, gripping the knob so hard it occurred to him it might snap off in his hand.

Chrissie appeared to be moving in slow motion as she gathered her purse and keys. She paused in front of him. "I wish there was something I could say—"

"Yeah, well, there's not. Just go."

He watched as she walked out the door, wanting nothing more than to slam it, but the damned spring hinge made that impossible. He closed his eyes, waiting for the sound of the latch clicking shut. Then reality hit him. He barely made it to the bathroom before he threw up.

Parker was still washing his face when Joey came in singing in an annoying falsetto voice and leaving a trail of shoes, backpack and soda cans like it was any other day.

"Getting ready for your hot weekend with Chrissie?"

Acid threatened to spew out of Parker again, but he managed to keep it together. *Breathe.* He glanced at the mirror, wondering how much of what he was struggling with showed on his face.

"Not going out with Chrissie." He walked into their room to find Joey sprawled on his bed, tossing a baseball against the wall.

"Finally came to her senses and dumped you, eh?"

Parker had the urge to pummel him. "She's getting married. To some guy who knocked her up."

It was the first time Parker had seen Joey drop a ball since they were six. Joey stared at him. "You're shitting me, right?"

Parker simply stared back. It hurt too much to say it again.

Joey shook his head. "Oh dude—"

There it was again. Pity. *Fuck.* Parker thumped down onto his bed.

"You all right?"

He knew this was Joey's idea of being compassionate. "Great."

"Sorry. Shit." Joey rummaged under the bed and came up with the ball. He bounced it off the wall again and the sound was comforting. "Well, you know what this means..."

"What, genius? What does this mean?"

"It means tonight you get to see how the other half lives. We're going out and we're gonna get you laid."

For the first time, Parker put up no argument. "Name the place. I'll be there."

Joey was working an early shift at MacDougal's so Parker agreed to meet him there. Driving down the street toward the pub, Parker tried to wrap his head around what had happened. *Pregnant. Married. How could she have done this?* He gripped the steering wheel so hard his knuckles shone white in the glow of the dashboard. The truck came out of nowhere. Parker saw light filling his Civic, heard the screech of tires, then metal crushing, glass shattering. Then nothing.

Chapter Three

Sophie had to keep herself from skipping all the way back to her house. Every last thing she'd remembered about Parker was still there—handsome, sweet, charming—but better. The last time she'd spent any real time with him, he'd still been teetering on the edge between adolescence and adulthood. That was no longer an issue. Parker was, without question, all man.

She shuddered, remembering the way the warmth of his laughter washed over her. The way he'd smiled when he realized it was her at the door. *Maybe now that we're older things will be different.* Hope filled her with a giddiness she hadn't felt since she'd found out Nate was cheating on her and wanted to end their two-month-old marriage. *Has Parker heard about that?*

For months she'd been unable to stop wondering who knew and who didn't. Finding out her husband had been cheating had been humiliating enough, but discovering that half the town knew before her had been even worse.

Sophie settled into her desk chair and turned on her laptop, watching as a dozen emails downloaded. Flower crisis. Cake decision. Wedding song. Being a party planner was her dream job. She loved making people's special days into dreams come true. But planning showers and weddings and engagement parties while going through a publically gossiped about divorce was another matter. Her clients had been great, for the most part. Only one had panicked and pulled out after hearing about her problems. The rest had stuck with her, and she'd worked extra hard to prove to herself and the rest of the world that her personal life hadn't broken her. It wasn't easy.

She answered every email, attaching photos and pasting in links, making sure each bride-to-be had everything she needed. As she hit send on the last one, she heard a tapping sound coming from the kitchen. No one ever knocked on the back door, especially past nine p.m. She peered around the doorway of her office. Through the French doors she could see the silhouette of a tall man. With a flutter that ran straight through her, she realized it was Parker.

Sophie combed her fingers through her hair, cursing the fact that she'd changed into a T-shirt and yoga pants when she'd gotten home. *Shit.* She wiped her fingers over her nose, hoping her face wasn't too shiny.

The rapping came again, and she realized if she didn't get to the door soon, he was going to leave. She turned the lock, still not believing Parker stood on her deck.

"Hey," he said. "Hope I'm not interrupting anything." His hair swept low over his eyes, and he looked sweet and shy. He looked like the boy she'd fallen in love with.

"Not at all. I just finished up some work."

A smile spread across Parker's face. "Well, in that case, you wanna have a beer?" He held up two bottles.

Grinning, Sophie nodded. "By the pool?"

"Sure." Parker stepped aside so she could join him on the deck.

The night air was warm and humid for early summer, the sky a deep blue from the last remnants of the sunset. "The water's not too cold. We could put our feet in."

"Okay." Parker kicked off his shoes and pulled off his socks then went to work cuffing up his jeans.

Sophie was already barefoot so she settled herself on the edge of the pool, dipping her feet into the cool water as she tugged her black yoga pants up above her knees. Parker lowered himself next to her, and she noticed another scar, this one running up the side of his muscular calf. Again he caught her staring. Her cheeks prickled, but Parker didn't do anything more than hold up one of the beers.

He twisted the cap off and handed it to her then opened his with a smirk. "You know half of me feels like we should be drinking these over in the shadows so your folks don't catch us."

Laughter tumbled out of Sophie. "I can't believe they never caught us."

"Do you think they knew and just didn't say anything?"

"My dad? Not say anything? No way. He thought I was a good girl."

Parker smiled. "You were a good girl. A good girl who could out drink her guy friends, but still a good girl."

She smacked him on the arm, stunned by how solid he felt beneath her hand. Her stomach flip-flopped.

"Sitting out here is my favorite thing about moving back to my parents' house."

"I can see why. Peaceful. And your landscaping looks great."

"Yeah," Sophie said. "I've been using this awesome company, Wood something or another... I've heard the owner's kinda cute." The minute the words left her mouth, she held her breath. *What's the matter with you?*

"Oh you've heard that, have you? He's probably a total ass."

"I don't think so." Sophie's heart beat irregularly. She sipped her beer, trying to keep from doing something stupid like going in for a kiss and inadvertently falling into the pool.

Parker took a long swallow of beer. Sitting by the pool with Sophie felt more normal—more enjoyable—than anything he'd done in the past two years. He'd never imagined it could feel so

27

good to just sit and talk to someone. Not that he didn't have other things on his mind. Watching her, with her dainty feet trailing across the water, her breasts straining against the soft fabric of her T-shirt, which brushed against his arm whenever she leaned toward him, it was as if he were sixteen again. Awkward and horny and wondering if she'd smack him if he tried to kiss her.

"Are you back at work already?" Sophie asked.

"Pretty much. I've been doing all the scheduling and books and stuff for the past six months while my dad was really sick."

Sadness filled Sophie's eyes, and he wanted to talk about anything else.

"I can't even imagine doing all that while you were still at the rehab center," she said.

"They were pretty great about it. I was there so long I knew damn near everyone. They'd even let me use their offices sometimes."

"I'm sure you charmed your way into whatever you needed."

She thinks I'm charming. A rush of heat coursed through him, settling in his groin. He wanted to reach out, to touch her, but he remained perfectly still. *Christ, I'm out of practice.* He took another swallow of beer.

Sophie bit her lip, drawing his full attention to the tempting swell of her mouth. Parker was about to speak when her cell phone interrupted with a loud buzzing that startled them both.

"Crap," Sophie said. "I have to get this. Work."

She hopped up, sending a delicate spray of water onto Parker's legs. He tried not to eavesdrop, but the sound of her voice was too alluring. "I promise, Kelsey, I'll get it all taken care of this weekend. I'll find you something perfect. No worries, okay?"

She paced back and forth while she talked, throwing Parker an eye roll and mouthing the word "Sorry".

He didn't mind. He'd wait all night to keep talking to her.

"Okay, Kels. I'll email you all the details, just enjoy your weekend." She hung up, slid the phone back into her pocket then seated herself alongside Parker again. A shiver ran through him when her leg brushed his as she slipped her feet back into the water.

"Everything okay?" he asked, trying to ignore the humming sensation that vibrated through him.

"Nervous bride. I'm going to a big trade show on Saturday, and she's dying to know if I find anything new and noteworthy." Sophie paused, running her fingers through the water. "Actually, I have an extra pass. You could come with...if you want."

"To a wedding show?" *Wait, did she just ask me out?*

"It's a gourmet food show—caterers, bakeries, importers—samples of everything. You basically eat your way through it. But you don't have to come. I mean, I know you don't really have any food at your house yet, I just thought..."

He loved the fact that she was rambling. She was nervous he'd say no. "Sounds great. I'd love to go."

Her eyes lit up. "Really?"

"Sure. What time?"

"It runs all day, but I like to go late morning so everyone's all set up but no one's run out of anything yet."

"Perfect. I just have to be back by four. Weekly date."

Her face fell. "Oh, okay. Sure. I can try to get an extra pass if you want to bring your girlfriend."

Girlfriend? It took him a second to realize that she'd assumed he meant he had a romantic date. "That won't be necessary. I just need to be on time. She gets pretty pissed if I'm late."

"If you can't come with me, that's okay. I mean, I don't want her to get mad or anything..."

Parker tried to keep as straight a face as possible. "Well, she *is* pretty controlling. We've been seeing each other about a year now, and she's adamant that we stick to our schedule. She's damn near impossible to please. Works me over so hard it hurts. And I pay her for it."

Sophie's eyes bugged. "You what?"

Parker let out a chuckle. "She's not my girlfriend. I see my physical therapist on Saturday afternoons. She's old enough to be my mom and she'd probably smack me in the head for giving you a hard time, but I couldn't help myself."

The scowl on Sophie's face made it impossible for him to keep from laughing. Somehow even with her lips pursed and her brow furrowed, she managed to look even more beautiful.

"You don't need your therapist to smack you. I'll take care of that." She swatted the back of his head the same way she used to when they were kids and one of his jokes pissed her off. And just like then, he liked the fact that she had any reason to put her hands on him.

He couldn't keep the grin off his face. "I told you the landscaping guy was an ass."

Chapter Four

"I'd better let you get some sleep," Parker said, though he didn't really want to leave.

Sophie glanced at her watch. "Oh my God, it's past midnight. I can't believe it's so late."

"Sorry."

"Don't be. I enjoyed the company." She glanced at her lap, and her hair fell across her face. Parker wanted to sweep it behind her shoulder, feel its silkiness beneath his fingers, draw her in for a slow, sweet kiss. Unsure if the moment was right, he resisted. He stood, extending a hand to help her up. Her warm, soft skin felt so inviting he rethought the kiss, but once again she looked down. *Shy? Or afraid I'm going to do something stupid like make a move when she doesn't want me to?* He felt sixteen again. *Jesus.*

"I should probably call the next time instead of just popping over."

Sophie's smile warmed him from head to toe. "You can call any time you want. Do you have your phone? I'll give you my number."

Parker patted his pockets. "Shit. I left it charging in the kitchen."

"Oh." Disappointment colored her lovely features.

"Here, I'll give you my number, and you can text me yours."

Her face brightened. He watched as her long fingers flew over the keyboard, typing in his name and number. "Done." The warm smile reappeared, as did Parker's desire to kiss her. "But you don't have to call to stop by. We'll do like we did when we were kids. If I'm home and up for company, I'll leave the back lights on."

Parker chuckled. "Only I won't have to worry about waking your parents and getting us both grounded."

Parker made his way back to his house. He couldn't remember the last time he'd laughed so much. His ribs were sore, his jaw ached and the heat that had concentrated below his waist for most of the evening was driving him insane. He traipsed up the stairs, stripping off his shirt as he went, unable to stop thinking about Sophie. He could still smell the sweet scent of her hair, could still hear the gentle vibrating tone of her laughter.

The freedom of being able to sleep in the nude was something he'd yet to get used to, but tonight he was particularly grateful for it. He stepped out of his jeans and boxers and fell into bed. The cool sheets felt refreshing against his overheated skin. After years of roommates and nurses, he finally had privacy. No need to sneak off to the bathroom and hope no one noticed how long he was gone. No worries about anyone overhearing.

He ran his hand down his stomach, feeling every nerve ending ignite in anticipation. His eyes closed, and Sophie filled his mind. This wasn't the first night that Sophie had unknowingly guest starred in his fantasies, but it was certainly among the more vivid. He stroked slowly, focusing on her image, the bow of her lips, the fullness of her breasts, the curve of her legs—imagining he was working his way over every inch of her.

A groan escaped him. He'd been achingly aroused for the better part of the past several hours, and now every sensation seemed magnified. Slowing his pace, he controlled his breathing, prolonging the anticipation. Pain had become such a prominent part of his life, he'd learned to make the most of pleasure.

He paused, giving himself a second to regain control. As much as he wanted to come he forced himself to wait, knowing the payoff would be that much sweeter if he did. The urgency faded, and he resumed stroking, drawing out each pass, wondering what it would be like if Sophie were there with him. Would she like things slow and sensual? Hot and fast? Would her touch be gentle? Forceful? Hungry? Imagining her hands on him, her nails skating across his skin, her body pressed to his, he gave in to the sensations and let them overtake him.

Sophie tried to sleep but found it impossible to quiet her mind. Parker had agreed to spend the day at the food show with her. Her pulse sped just thinking about it. *Is this a date? Or is he lonely and thinks this is a friendly afternoon outing?*

She'd been on a half-dozen dates since her divorce had been finalized, and not one of them had inspired her to accept a second invitation. Some were nicer than others, but none had held her interest. Talking to Parker was an entirely different matter. In spite of the years they'd gone without seeing each other, it felt like no time had passed. The easy comfort between them was prominent. The old attraction burned even hotter than she remembered.

What the hell was Chrissie thinking letting him go? Sophie didn't have the details but she'd heard enough through the town's gossip mill. As rushed as Chrissie's wedding had been, it had been widely assumed that the marriage was necessary because she was pregnant. Her minister father had tried to downplay the rampant chatter, but everyone knew.

Parker's "accident" had been questioned as well. Had it truly been the other driver's fault, or had he been reckless on purpose?

A shiver ran through Sophie. The mere thought of Parker trying to hurt himself, over Chrissie no less, was more than she could stand. He deserved so much better. Always had. Someone who could appreciate him. Who would never hurt him. *Someone like me.* The thought disappeared as quickly as it came, leaving a trail of emptiness in its wake. *He never wanted me. Not that way.*

Sighing, she got out of bed and headed to the kitchen to get a drink. The cool water settled the flushed feeling that had her unsettled. Her gaze drifted across the yard to Parker's house. Not a light shone from any window. *At least one of us is getting some sleep tonight.* The two days until the food show seemed like an eternity. *Maybe it's time to make that casserole.*

Chapter Five

Parker awoke in a cold sweat, heart racing, unable to catch his breath. Shadows of trees waved deep gray lines across the blue walls of the room. His pulse slowed as he realized he was home.

"Jesus," he said, raking his hands through his hair, focusing on breathing. *Will they ever stop?* Nightmares had plagued him since the accident. Always different but variations on the same theme. Pain. Fear. Confusion. Helplessness. All his least favorite things magnified and rolled into one.

The hot, stuffy air of his bedroom did nothing to stop his shivering as the sweat evaporated off his bare skin. He yanked on a T-shirt and boxers. The first step out of bed reminded him that he had to go see Tanya. A jolt of pain shot down his right thigh. As he walked down the stairs, he felt the stiffness in his legs begin to loosen as the tension ebbed.

Only the hint of a sunrise warmed the sky, leaving the kitchen dark. He flipped on the small light above the stove, and his eyes were immediately drawn to the cake platter. His stomach rumbled as he cut a thick slice and placed it on a plate. The first forkful filled his mouth with creamy sweetness, bringing his thoughts straight to Sophie.

Even when he'd been dating Chrissie, his main regret had been what their relationship had done to his friendship with Sophie.

"I don't think Chrissie likes you hanging out with me," she'd said to him on more than one occasion.

"Well, she'll need to get over that," Parker had always answered. They'd continued to spend time together, but it had never been quite the same. They'd even double dated when Sophie had a boyfriend, but then Parker was the one who was uncomfortable. Feeling protective of Sophie came as naturally as breathing, and he'd never liked the guys she dated.

"You're worse than a big brother," she'd told him.

"I worry about you, that's all." He was never sure if that argument was to convince her or himself, because he knew all along that it was more than that. He'd felt jealous even though he knew he'd had no right to.

Joey had called him on it a bunch of times. "Shit, she's not your girlfriend. Take a pill. Does Chrissie know you've got a boner for your best friend?"

"I don't want her to get hurt."

Joey had laughed. "Yeah, okay. Just tell me one thing—you use your right hand or your left while you're coming up with these rationalizations?"

It all seemed foolish in retrospect. In spite of all the time he'd spent feeling guilty about his closeness with Sophie, he'd never once cheated on Chrissie—with anyone. He'd been faithful. Loyal. *And what did it get me?* He took another forkful of cake. *What's done is done. This time I'm going after what I want.* And what he wanted was Sophie. More than he'd ever wanted anything.

Parker spent the day in the home office, going through contracts. As a kid he'd hated working on projects for the family business, but while he was recovering, he'd appreciated having something to focus on and had grown to like it. The financial end came easily—he'd always had a head for numbers—but the design end came as a pleasant surprise.

The digital programs had taken some time to learn, but once he had, he found that he liked drawing up virtual plans for landscapes. He had a knack for listening to what people wanted and turning their ideas into designs that worked. And he certainly didn't mind that every contract he'd signed lately was for over $30,000. One of the first orders of business when he started going into the office would be hiring another crew. With summer here, it was the only way to keep up with the demand.

You'd be happy, Dad. We're going to have a great season. Honoring his dad's memory was as important to Parker as proving to himself that he could be successful even without the baseball career he'd planned for his entire life. Wood Landscaping was now his future, and he intended to make the most of it. He was still at his desk when his phone buzzed. He found it buried under the plans for the renovations on the Davis Country Club's outdoor sitting area. He'd been expecting a text from the stone company but when he clicked on his phone he saw Sophie's name instead. His mood brightened.

In case your fridge is still empty I thought I'd let you know I made lasagna for dinner.

A smile spread across his face as he typed.

It's kinda mean to brag about lasagna to a starving guy.

He imagined the flustered look on her face and chuckled, staring at his phone.

sigh I was offering for you to have some lasagna, but if you're gonna be a wiseass about it, I don't know...

The smile widened into a grin.

I'll behave. I promise. Want me to bring some wine?

I've got plenty of wine, just come over whenever you're ready.

I'm always ready for lasagna. Be right there.

Parker caught a whiff of tomato sauce the second he stepped onto her back porch. His stomach rumbled as he breathed in the rich, tempting aroma that wafted through the open windows. Then he saw her and forgot all about food.

Sophie stood at the kitchen counter, her back to the door, drizzling olive oil into a small bowl. Her hands danced across the spice rack as she plucked out several jars. Her amber hair cascaded over one shoulder, leaving the other side of her neck bare. She reached for a potholder and pulled open the oven door, bending over and giving Parker a heart-stopping view.

Her shorts curved enticingly around her full hips and revealed long, smooth legs. She set a bubbling pan of lasagna on top of the stove and wiped her cheek with the back of her hand. Every move she made enthralled him. He wanted to come up behind her, nuzzle the curve of her neck, breathe in her sweet scent, press himself against the soft swell of her hips.

His thoughts were interrupted as she turned to face him. A smile spread across her face as she strode to the door.

"Perfect timing," she said, holding the door open.

Sophie's cheeks flushed and she couldn't tell if it was from the heat in the kitchen or the look on Parker's face. *How long was he at the door? Was he watching me?* The fluttery feeling returned.

"I can't remember the last time I had lasagna. It smells amazing."

Sophie went back to making the salad, feeling the need to keep her hands busy. "I'm guessing the food wasn't great at the center?"

"That would be a serious understatement. It made memories of the college cafeteria seem gourmet in comparison."

"I wish I'd have known that. I'd have brought you food."

Parker's grin lit up his whole face. "That would have been awesome."

Sophie bit her lip, focusing on slicing a tomato. "I tried to visit you once, you know. Right after the accident. Your dad said you didn't want to see anyone."

"I don't remember him telling me that you came by, but he might have. I was pretty heavily drugged at first but I do remember refusing to have visitors."

Sophie's gaze darted to Parker as she tried to gauge how comfortable he was with the topic. "Why?"

He shrugged, his fingers sweeping his hair off his face for a second before it fell back across his forehead. "I was a disaster. In every way imaginable. I didn't even want to deal with myself let alone anyone else." He paused and ran his hand along the edge of the counter. "I hated seeing that look in everyone's eyes."

Sophie's chest clenched, trapping the air in her lungs. "What look?"

His eyes met hers, distractingly blue and intense. "Pity."

She exhaled. "I know exactly what you mean. That's the look I got from everyone when I got divorced."

"Never thought about that."

She tossed the tomatoes into the salad and started whisking the dressing. "Trust me. When everyone in town knows your husband's cheating on you before you know, you get the pity face everywhere you go."

"That's why you got divorced?" The surprise on his face told her he hadn't heard the rumors, and she regretted having blurted it out. *Way to make yourself desirable. Shit.*

"Yeah."

"What a dick."

Sophie laughed and handed him the salad. "No argument there."

His strong fingers grasped the bowl. "Seriously, Soph. Any guy who cheats on his wife is an asshole. And any guy who'd cheat on you is a fucking idiot."

His words sent a warm tremor straight through her. "Thanks."

"Just being honest."

Sophie carried the lasagna pan to the table. "Can you grab the bread?"

Parker picked up the cutting board and pulled a knife out of the butcher block.

Watching as he sliced the crusty Italian bread into thick, even slices, Sophie tried to imagine how hard it must have been for him not to be able to do anything for himself for so long. "I wouldn't have pitied you."

"What?" His eyes darted to hers again, dark brows furrowed.

"I wouldn't have pitied you," she repeated, to make sure he heard her. "I knew you'd be strong enough to recover. I just would have kept you company. And brought you real food."

The shy smile spread across his face again, giving her another glimpse of the boy she'd fallen for so many years ago. "Then I guess I really am too stubborn for my own good. I'd probably have gotten better twice as fast with medicinal lasagna."

"I'll give you an extra-large serving to make up for lost time."

Chapter Six

Sophie could barely concentrate at work the next day. Her thoughts kept drifting back to Parker. They'd had a perfect night together—talking until past midnight, eating and drinking wine. But when he'd gotten up to leave, things had turned awkward. He'd kept his hands shoved in his pockets, rocking on his heels as they said good night. She'd wanted a kiss so badly she thought she might pass out, but she had no idea what else to do to let him know. The last thing she wanted was to make him feel uncomfortable or, worse, have him reject her. That she couldn't handle.

"What's gotten into you today? That's the third time you've asked me about the Carter wedding. The invoice went out last week." Cindy, her business manager planted her hand on her hip and squinted as if she could read Sophie's thoughts if she looked hard enough.

"Sorry. I'm just distracted." Sophie slumped against her chair.

"It's that guy, isn't it?" Cindy's always-round eyes widened more than seemed possible, and she perched on the edge of Sophie's desk. "Talk to me."

She thought about denying it, but there was no point. Cindy had known her for five years—first as college roommates then as business partners. There was no way she could successfully keep anything from her. "Yes."

"I knew it." Cindy wiggled her shoulders from side to side the way she always did when she was proud of herself. "So, what's the deal? Has he asked you out yet?"

"No." Sophie groaned and put her head down on the desk. "Actually, I think I asked him out."

"You think?"

"He's coming with me to the food show. I don't know if it's a date or not."

"But you want it to be."

Sophie gave Cindy her most condescending look, which she knew wasn't particularly convincing.

Cindy laughed. "He said yes, right? He obviously wants to spend time with you. That's got to be a good sign."

"True. But it may just be friend time."

"Even if it is now, that can change."

Sophie burrowed her face into her arm and groaned. "I know."

"Wow. You really like this guy."

"Since we were kids."

"Well, I hope he's worth the wait. You deserve a good guy for a change. In the meantime, you need to perk up. The Hendersons will be here in fifteen minutes, and you need to dazzle them with your presentation."

"Shit. You're right." *Focus. What's wrong with you?*

"I'm always right." Cindy hopped off the desk and darted away before Sophie could smack her. "And if this Parker dude has any sense, he'll make a move on you this weekend. Mark my words."

Sophie rolled her eyes but couldn't help hoping that Cindy was right.

Chapter Seven

The intricate displays at the food show contained the most elaborate culinary concoctions Parker had ever seen. Towering pyramids of cream puffs housed in structures sculpted out of chocolate. Fruits and vegetables carved into flowers or turned into edible cups containing anything from savory soups to the lightest mousses he'd ever tasted. Bite-sized samples of everything from cheese to candied nuts to grilled meats. Each table more impressive than the last.

As much as he enjoyed the food, all of it paled in comparison to how happy it made him to spend the day with Sophie. She'd been a whirlwind since they'd first entered the expo. It seemed as though she knew at least half of the vendors, most of whom had come out from behind their displays to greet her with a hug or a kiss before pulling her to the side to give her special samples they'd held aside for VIPs. Impressive and more than a little bit of a turn on. Parker knew Sophie as the smart, capable, sweet girl she'd been when they were younger, but he'd never seen her in work mode. Her charm and grace were irresistible. And clearly not just to him.

"You're certainly popular with this crowd," he said, taking the umpteenth box of chocolates out of her hand so she could finish eating the miniature key lime mousse cup she'd just plucked off a silver tray.

Her auburn brows pinched together. "What do you mean?"

Watching her pop the last of the mousse cup into her mouth and lick a stray crumb from the corner of her lips made Parker's abdominal muscles tense. He held up the three large totes full of samples they'd accumulated. "Do you not realize how many freebies we've got here?"

She grinned, sending the tension lower. "Okay, so maybe a few of them favor me a little bit."

"They love you."

Her cheeks pinked. "Half of them probably just wanted a closer look at the hot guy who's carrying my bags."

Hot guy? That's got to be good. "So you're saying you brought me along just to snag extra giveaways?"

"Pretty much. And so I wouldn't have to carry them myself." She batted her eyelashes, her lips pursed in a coquettish grin.

He wanted to drop all the bags, sweep her into his arms and kiss her right there in the center of the dessert aisle.

"Oh, Antoinette's Chocolates. You have to try her truffles. They're insane."

She curled her fingers around the crook of his arm and tugged him toward a table with a white chocolate Eiffel tower. Having her hand on him made Parker even less able to concentrate on the food. He could imagine her hands everywhere. *Is she just being friendly or does she want to touch me as much as I want to touch her?*

His thoughts were interrupted as she held a small chocolate pyramid to his lips. "Try this."

He swallowed hard then opened his mouth. Sophie popped in the chocolate. Her fingertips brushed his lips, making him feel lightheaded from lack of blood flow to his brain. He forced himself to chew the candy. The creamy chocolate liquefied on contact with his tongue, releasing a combination of caramel and hazelnut. "God, that's good."

"Mmmm." She closed her eyes as she chewed. "They're my absolute favorites. I shouldn't admit this but I try to talk clients into ordering them just so I'll get to eat them at the wedding."

"Do you go to every wedding?"

She nodded, her eyes scanning the display. "Pretty much. Here. These are amazing too." Again her delicate fingers paused in front of his lips, this time holding up a disc of chocolate with a white-chocolate rose etched on the surface.

Caramel and sea salt flooded his mouth as soon as he bit into the dark chocolate shell. "Jesus. I've got to get myself invited to some weddings. This stuff's amazing."

Sophie laughed, the shimmery sound sending tingles through Parker's limbs. "Or you can be extra nice to me, and maybe I'll bring you home goodie bags from all the ones I go to."

She grabbed two sample boxes off the table and tucked them into one of the tote bags.

Parker chuckled. "Now there's officially more food in these bags than in my entire kitchen."

"That's just because I haven't taken you grocery shopping yet. We'll get your kitchen stocked soon enough."

"Sounds good." Anything that involved more time with Sophie sounded good. His gaze was drawn to the saunter of her hips as she made her way through the crowd. *Jesus.*

"I think we've hit every booth. You ready to go?"

"Sure."

Parker held the door as they left the convention center. As they headed down the street, the sky darkened with deep blue clouds. Thunder rumbled long and deep. "Think we'll make it to the car before the storm starts?"

No sooner did the words leave his mouth than the sky opened up.

Sophie shrieked, "No. Run."

They tore down the sidewalk, fat raindrops pelting them faster by the second. One of Sophie's sandals slipped off, and she started giggling. "Wait, my shoe."

Parker stopped, slicking his hair back off his face. "Got it?"

"No." She laughed harder, grabbing Parker's arm to steady herself as she wiggled her foot back into the shoe. "There."

Her eyes sparkled as she gazed up at him, her breath coming fast from laughter, her rain-soaked shirt clinging to her every curve. Parker smoothed her wet hair off her cheek. The feel of her skin, warm and inviting, was too much. He couldn't wait another second.

His lips touched hers mid-giggle, for just a second. He held his breath, his fingers still woven into her hair, waiting to see if she'd pull away. She hesitated, the sweet scent of her making him dizzy, then her mouth was back on his.

Sophie went up on her toes, leaning in toward him, her lips parting beneath his. She tasted like the chocolate they'd had and red wine they hadn't, a decadent blend of the richest flavors he'd ever savored. He no longer noticed the rain or heard the thunder—his whole world had condensed into the kiss. The only word his brain could form was *Sophie*.

I'm kissing Parker. Sophie repeated the words to herself but couldn't quite believe they were true. His hand left her face, and she instantly missed his touch until she realized he was just moving it lower. A strong arm curled around her waist, drawing her closer. Broad chest pressing against hers. Hips rocking into her. Tongue. Oh, God, velvety soft tongue circling hers. Words ceased to exist as she rode the mind-numbing swirls into a blissful oblivion.

His lips closed, brushing hers once more. "It's still raining."

"I hadn't noticed." She was breathless enough that the words came out as a whisper.

She caught the quick grin that passed over his face before his mouth returned to hers. *Holy shit.* She'd always imagined he'd kiss well but nothing like this had ever even entered her fantasies. Gentle yet hungry, subtle but commanding. She moved in toward him, somewhat dizzily aware of the fact that he was hard. Her heart beat so fast she was sure he could feel it through their drenched clothes.

"We'd better get to the car." His voice startled her, and she realized her eyes were still closed.

Shaking her head, she felt the heavy, water-soaked tips of hair hitting her cheek. "Okay." She'd have agreed to pretty much anything he suggested at that point. All she really wanted was another moment with his mouth on hers.

"Come on." Parker held out his hand, and she slipped her fingers into his.

He's holding my hand. Her fourteen-year-old self did a happy twirl in her head. Her twenty-four-year-old self felt more excited than she had in... When was the last time she felt this? Heat flooded her face. Breathless, she ran with him through the rainy streets until they finally reached the car.

Parker opened her door, and she climbed in, tossing her purse into the backseat. Watching in the rear-view mirror, she saw him open the hatch and stow the bags. *God he looks good soaking wet.*

The door slammed shut, and Parker trotted to the front of the car, swinging into the seat next to her. His shirt clung to the muscles of his chest, his hair dripped. *This must be what he looks like in the shower.* She felt her cheeks tingle, realizing she was picturing him naked.

"You okay?" he asked, raking his hair off his face, beads of rain still clinging to his long dark lashes.

Nodding, she tried to focus on getting the keys in the ignition. "You?"

"I'm great."

She turned to find him looking at her with a smile she'd never seen before. His eyes were dark and expectant, twinkling

Karen Stivali

at her like two mischievous sapphires. Tumbling over its own beats, her heart danced a jig.

The rain continued, battering the car in solid sheets as she made her way home. By the time they pulled into her driveway it was nearly three thirty. "Sorry we got back so late. Are you going to make it to your appointment?"

"It's right in town. I'll be fine." He got out of the car and opened the hatch.

"I've got it, you go. I don't want to make you late."

Grabbing the tote bags, he laughed. "Will you please just get in the house?"

Sophie fiddled with the keys until she found the right one. She held the door, sneaking a look at Parker's clingy shirt from behind as he moved past her. The defined muscles of his back looked just as tempting as his chest. Not to mention his ass. *Get a hold of yourself, will you?*

"Good thing these bags are waterproof, or all those samples would have turned into soup." He set the bags on the kitchen counter.

"What? Oh, yeah." Free samples were the last thing on her mind. She wished he didn't have to go.

"Thanks for taking me to the show. It was great."

Great didn't begin to cover it. "Anytime." *Say something else.* Her brain refused to function.

"I better get going or I really will be late."

"Oh, okay. Sure." *Think, dammit.*

Parker headed back to the door.

"Do you want to borrow an umbrella?" *Brilliant. Very seductive. How can he possibly resist a come-on like that?*

"You can only get so wet, and I think I'm there."

You and me both. She held her breath, hoping she hadn't said that out loud.

48

Parker reached for the handle of the screen door then paused. "I'll be done with PT by six—do you want to grab dinner later?"

There was nothing she'd rather do but she shook her head. "I can't. I've got to meet with one of my clients tonight. Her fiancé lives out of state, and this is the only time they're both available before the wedding."

"Okay." Parker's eyes shifted away from hers.

"But I'm free tomorrow night."

The smile that curved across his lips sent a tugging sensation from her heart straight to her thighs. "Tomorrow's great. It's a date. How's six o'clock?"

"Perfect." *A date.* She had to keep from bouncing on her toes.

He leaned in and gave her a soft kiss that left her feeling completely devoid of oxygen. "See you then."

Nodding, she watched as he stepped back out into the downpour and jogged toward his house. *I have a date with Parker. What the hell do you wear on a first date with the guy you've been pining after for over a decade?*

Chapter Eight

Parker stripped off his wet clothes and changed into sweatpants and a T-shirt. Rushing so he wouldn't be late, he trotted out to his car, glad that it was now only drizzling.

"What's got you in such a good mood?" Tanya asked the second she walked into the treatment room.

"What do you mean?" Parker asked, unable to keep what he imagined was a completely goofy grin off his face.

"That." Tanya circled her finger in the air in front of him. Her eyes narrowed as she studied him. "Generally speaking, that look only means one thing. What's her name?"

Chuckling, Parker lay down on the table, staring at the ceiling tiles to avoid Tanya's eyes.

"I can hurt you, you know," she said.

"Oh, I know." Parker laughed. "Fine. Her name's Sophie."

"That's pretty. And where did you meet Sophie?" Tanya's hands began to work down his leg, bending it at the knee.

"JFK Elementary School."

Tanya's mouth dropped open. "You're young, kid, but you're not that young."

"I was when I met her. We grew up together."

"Mmmm, interesting. Childhood sweetheart?"

Parker's stomach tensed, partly from the pulling muscles in his thigh and partly from thoughts of Chrissie. "No. Childhood buddy. But I always sort of had a thing for her."

"Nice." She pressed down hard, crossing his knee over his other leg.

Grimacing, Parker tried to focus on the conversation. "It is. We've been hanging out since I moved back to my dad's. She's awesome. We get along great. When we're together, it's just like it was when we were younger. Like no time has passed."

"I love friendships like that. But now I guess you're more than friends?"

Parker smiled and nodded. "We've got a date tomorrow night."

Tanya sighed. "I miss dating. Marriage really fucks that up."

"You kill me."

"Not yet. Roll over, we'll see what I can do."

Parker braced his arms on the narrow table and flipped onto his stomach. "Give it your best shot."

"I intend to. Though I don't want you too sore for date night."

Parker's breath caught in his chest. *Date night.* He hadn't had anything remotely resembling a date in over two years. Not to mention that he'd never really dated anyone but Chrissie. *Jesus. What the fuck do I even do on a date?*

"You have a favorite restaurant? Or, you know, one you'd like to go to if you ever dated anymore?" he asked.

"Depends what you mean by favorite. You want fun and casual? Or fancy favorite?"

I have no idea. "How about telling me both?"

"Well, for casual I like Kelsey's Pub. Good burgers, live music most nights, but it's a little noisy—not great for talking. For fancy I like La Cippolina. Cozy little tables, candlelight, crazy-good food."

What's better for a first date? He didn't want to look like an idiot and ask. "If you could only go to one, which do you like better?"

"Are you trying to impress her?"

Tanya's hand dug into a particularly sore spot on his hip, and he grunted, gritting his teeth against the pain. "I just want to have a good time." *Understatement. I want this to be perfect.*

"Why don't you start with Kelsey's. It's nice and relaxed. If you get a second date out of her, then you can impress her with a night at La Cippolina."

"Thanks." *If?* He tried to breathe deeply and not tense as she pressed harder, kneading a knot.

"That's why you pay me the big bucks. But since I'm helping with the plans, I'm gonna expect details on Monday."

"You always expect details."

"Good point." She touched a spot that made Parker see stars. He clenched his eyes tightly, inhaling deeply through his nose, and attempted to let thoughts of Sophie carry him away.

"On your left side." Tanya patted his hip and he rolled to the side, trying not to cringe from the intensified ache. "You nervous?"

Shit, is it that obvious? "Not exactly."

Tanya's raised eyebrow spoke volumes as she stared right into his eyes.

Parker sighed. "Fine. A little. I haven't been on a date in years."

"I'm pretty sure they haven't changed much."

"Probably not. But I haven't had a first date since high school."

"Breathe deep." Tanya positioned herself alongside him, and he knew she was getting ready to stretch the tightest muscles in his leg.

Drawing in a slow, steady breath, he realized how nervous he really was. Forget butterflies, it felt like he had bats circling in his stomach. Remembering the kiss they'd shared was the only thing keeping him from totally freaking.

Kisses. More than one. It had felt so good to kiss someone. *No. Not just someone. To kiss her.* To have her in his arms.

"You'll do great, Parker. What woman in her right mind wouldn't want to be with you?"

Chrissie.

"Whoa, kid. What just happened? You knotted up from head to toe." Tanya's hand stilled. "Back on your stomach. We need you more relaxed before we work on the leg."

Parker positioned himself on the table, his face nestled in the cutaway cushion. He closed his eyes and heard her step aside and pump more goop onto her hands.

"Talk to me," she said. "We're not gonna be able to finish this session until you can relax a little, so whatever it is, spit it out."

Parker took a deep breath, flinching as she smoothed the icy gel over his skin. He opened his mouth, but the words that were choking him couldn't come out. "It's nothing," he managed to say.

Tanya snorted. "You want me to guess?"

"Not really."

"Let's see if I can guess." She worked her hands in a circular pattern across his back, pressing hard, forcing him to loosen up, even though he felt himself fighting her. "You're friends already, so you must be sure she likes you. You care where you're taking her, so obviously you like her. You worried about the sex?"

Parker's face flooded with heat. He remained silent.

"I'll take that as a yes. Don't worry about that. It's like riding a bicycle. You won't have forgotten."

Swallowing hard and squeezing his eyes shut, Parker braced himself against the pressure of Tanya's hands as the icy sensation turned to heat. "You can't forget something you never knew."

Her hands froze for a second, and he knew she was processing what he said. His face burned hotter than the goop on his back. She started rubbing again, concentrating on a knot deep in his shoulder where he tended to carry the most tension. "Never?"

He shook his head from side to side, certain he was ironing the sheet beneath him with the heat radiating from his face.

"Weren't you and that other girl engaged?"

Tanya dug her fingers into a spot so tight Parker grunted, but focusing on the pain made it easier to talk. "Yep. Minister's daughter. Wanted to wait 'til we were married."

"Jesus."

"Yep, it's Jesus's fault."

Tanya laughed. "Good one. How long were you two together?"

"Four years." As painful as it was to discuss, Parker felt some of the tension draining out of him. Keeping a secret that big had weighed on him more than he realized. Humiliating as it was to admit, at least someone knew. And she hadn't fallen over in a dead faint or anything.

"You're a good guy. I know a lot who wouldn't have agreed to wait."

"I know. Like the one she cheated on me with." *Might as well make the humiliation complete.*

"Look, Park, this is all in the past. Focus on your life now. If Sophie's as awesome as you're telling me she is, she's not going to care."

"I just don't want to be... I don't want to screw up." His heart pounded against the massage table hard enough he could count the beats.

"Screw up the sex? First off there are plenty of guys with tons of experience who screw up sex. Women are used to that, so right there—please—take some pressure off yourself. Are you worried you're not gonna know what to do? I mean, without prying too much, did you and your ex do anything? Or not at all?"

Parker sighed, digging his forehead farther into the face cushion, beyond grateful that this had all come up during a facedown part of the treatment. "We did some stuff. Not a lot. And she was never really that into it."

Tanya moved back down toward Parker's thigh. He wasn't sure if she thought he'd relaxed enough that she could work on it or if she sensed that he needed the distraction of more pain to keep up the conversation.

As she stretched the damaged muscle, she continued. "It doesn't matter, really. Every woman is different. Any time you're with someone new, you have to discover what works for her. That's true for any guy. Trust me on that. Even the ones who think they've got it all figured out—half the time they don't. They just think they do. Biggest mistake guys make is rushing. Don't rush things. Go slow."

"What do you mean?"

Tanya paused then went back to stretching his leg. "It's kind of like massage. A good therapist doesn't just go straight to work on the trouble spot, they get to know the person's body. I always tell you I could do this job blind because I see with my hands. A good lover sees with his hands."

That makes sense. "Okay."

"Take your time. Women like to be touched. All over, not just on the naughty bits."

Parker breathed out a laugh then groaned as Tanya bent his leg at the knee then tugged it down, stretching the sore ligaments to their fullest reach.

"And ask her questions. Most guys don't do that, but they should."

"What kind of questions?"

"Simple things like 'does that feel good?' You'd be surprised how many women will let a guy keep doing something that feels awful because they don't want to tell him he's doing it wrong and make him feel bad. If you ask, you're giving her the opportunity to tell you and maybe show you how to do it the way she prefers it."

Oh Jesus. The thought of doing stuff wrong filled him with a dread so heavy he felt like he could sink right through the table from the weight of it. "Okay."

"Just pay attention. The fact that you're worried about it means you care, and that right there gives you a huge advantage over half the guys out there. Seriously. You'll do fine." She took her hands off his leg, and he heard her wiping them on a towel. "Lay there for a few minutes and rest. I worked you kind of hard today."

Parker was thankful to be able to stay face down until she left the room. "Thanks."

"No problem." She reached over and ruffled the back of his hair. "Have fun on your date. Just be yourself and remember, she's a lucky girl."

Lucky? We'll see.

Chapter Nine

Sophie looked in the hall mirror for at least the fifth time since she'd gotten dressed for her date with Parker. Turning from side to side, she reached under her short black skirt to tug her top down farther. *Does this lay flat enough? Should I wear a sweater instead?* She pulled at the fabric beneath her arms, trying to make sure she wasn't getting too sweaty. *Calm. Down.* She forced a smile so she could make sure there was no lipstick on her teeth. *It's just Parker. We've hung out a million times.* Her attempt at being rational failed. The word "date" bounced around her mind like a pinball.

The sound of Parker's car pulling into her driveway made her jump. Glancing quickly in the mirror one last time, she tucked her hair behind her ears. *You can do this.* The doorbell rang, and she tried to relax. Seeing him standing on her front steps—dark trousers, a shirt as blue as his eyes, dark hair styled but still pleasantly tousled—it was all she could do to keep from grabbing his arm, pulling him into the house and pinning him to the nearest wall.

God help me. "Hey," she said, afraid any other attempt at speaking might lead to her saying something crazy like "take me now".

A toe-curling smile spread across Parker's face. "You look great."

An intense flush filled her cheeks, making them prickle. "Thanks."

Grabbing her purse and keys, she stepped outside into the humid air. Parker held the car door open for her, and she climbed up into the soft leather seats. He slid into the driver's seat, and she watched his hand as he started the car. Long, strong fingers. She loved looking at his fingers. Loved imagining what they'd feel like against her skin. A shudder rippled through her, and she tried to pretend she was adjusting her seat belt so he wouldn't notice.

Parker backed out of the driveway, giving her a quick glance that made her tremble again. "How'd your meetings go?"

"Great. The couple I met with today liked some of the samples I brought home from the show, so I actually wrapped up an event."

"Awesome. What'd they pick?"

"They want the chocolate pyramids as their wedding favors."

Parker let out a moan that made Sophie squirm in her seat. "Those were insane. I think every wedding should hand those out."

Giggling, she studied Parker's profile. Straight, narrow nose, impossibly sculpted jaw. He'd shaved, which made his skin look so smooth and irresistible she had to stop herself from reaching out to stroke his cheek.

He caught her staring. "What?"

You're gorgeous. "Just thinking about how you look. You look the same and different at the same time."

He breathed out a laugh, turning his head to give her a quick look up and down again. "So do you."

"God, I hope not. I was such a geek in high school."

Parker's eyebrows shot up. "Geek? No. You were smart but you were never a geek."

"Come on, Parker. It's okay. I know I was."

"I was there too, you know. And you weren't. You were always cute. At least I thought so."

You did? Her heart sputtered. "Did not."

"Do you remember your birthday party in ninth grade?"

Sophie tucked her leg underneath her so she could sit facing Parker. "Yeah."

"And it was so cold no one else was in the pool, except me."

"I remember that. My mom kept telling you to get out. You were turning blue. But you insisted on staying in."

Parker nodded. "Yeah, well there's a reason I dove into that cold water. When you walked out of your house in that black bathing suit..."

Sophie's breath caught in her throat. She remembered the suit. It was the first sexy bathing suit her mom had ever let her buy. She'd been super self-conscious about wearing it, but her friends had convinced her. "I was so scared to wear that suit."

"Well, I was scared everyone was gonna see my reaction to you wearing that suit, and the only thing I could think to do was jump in the pool."

"Seriously?" Sophie giggled, having a hard time believing him.

"Do you have any idea how cold that water was?"

"I do. I'd stuck my foot in right before the party and was totally bummed because I knew no one would go in."

"Then that should give you an idea of how much I needed to cool off after seeing you."

Sophie couldn't stop grinning. "Thanks for telling me that."

"I can't believe I just did. I'm just trying to make a point. You were not a geek in high school, no matter what you might have thought."

Sophie looked down, unsure of how to respond. Parker reached over and picked up her hand. The feel of his fingers sliding over hers warmed her. His fingertips grazed hers gently, sending tremors up her arm. She stroked his palm, and he linked his fingers with hers, closing around them. It was such a simple gesture. *He's just holding my hand. Why does it feel like my heart is going to burst?* They rode in silence until he pulled into the parking lot at Kelsey's.

"I didn't know we were coming here," she said.

"Is that okay?" Parker looked worried.

"It's great. The Blue Moons are playing tonight. I book them for weddings a lot. They're an awesome cover band."

"Good." Parker gave her hand a quick squeeze before letting go. She missed his touch immediately. *Get a grip, would you?*

There was a small crowd of people at the doorway but Parker ushered her past them, his hand on her lower back in a way that made her feel dizzy. *I'm not going to survive the night at this rate.*

The waitress seated them at a booth slightly off to the side of the room so they had a little privacy but were close enough to the stage that they'd still be able to see the band. "Have you been here before?" Sophie asked.

Parker shook his head. "No. You?"

"All the time. The owner used to work at one of the catering halls I use a lot."

"Is there anyone you don't know?"

Sophie felt her cheeks burn again. "Sorry. I don't mean to be name dropping."

"No, I think it's awesome. You're amazing. Your business. The way people respond to you. I'm so proud of you."

Proud of me? Sophie couldn't remember the last time anyone had said they were proud of her. The divorce had made her feel like the disgrace of the family. She tried not to think about it but she knew her divorce had been the deciding factor in her parents moving down to Florida two years before they'd planned to go.

And her ex. He'd been anything but proud of her career. He'd all but blamed her job for causing their marriage to fail. "Maybe if you'd been working on our marriage as much as you work on other people's, I wouldn't have been alone so much and I wouldn't have cheated."

"You okay?" Parker touched her hand, and the tingle returned.

Nodding, she smoothed her fingers against his. "I'm better than I've been in a while."

Sophie saw Laura, an old classmate and notorious busybody, making her way to their table, menus in hand. Her eyes widened as she approached them. "Oh my God, Parker. I thought that was you."

"Hey, Laura. Wow, it's been a long time."

"You look great. When did you get back in town?"

"A few days ago."

Sophie tried to gauge his reaction. He seemed a little uncomfortable.

"I was real sorry to hear about your dad."

Parker's expression remained unchanged, with the same smile on his face as he nodded, but Sophie noticed his eyes darken, his posture tighten. *Just give us our menus, would you, Laura?*

"Thanks," Parker said.

"Hey, we should all go out for drinks some time. Like the old days, right, Soph? It's so funny seeing you two together again." She placed the menus on the table. "I'll tell Nick you're here."

Sophie tried to say no, but Laura had already darted away from the table. *Shit.* Sophie had been flirting with Nick for months, hoping he'd ask her out. He wasn't serious dating material, but he'd been a great distraction when she'd first gotten divorced. Sweet. Sexy. Easy on the eyes. And always ready to shower her with the attention she'd desperately craved right after Nate had left her. Tonight, however, the last thing she wanted was a flirty conversation with another guy.

"Who's Nick?" Parker asked.

As her mind raced to come up with the best answer, Nick Calabra strode toward them with a huge grin on his handsome face.

"He's the chef." She managed to get out before Nick bent down and kissed her on the cheek, pulling her into a half hug.

"Where've you been hiding, Soph? Haven't seen you in a few weeks."

"Just busy working."

Nick glanced at Parker, and Sophie realized she'd better introduce them. "Nick I'd like you to meet my..." *Oh shit. My what? It's way too soon to say boyfriend.* "...friend, Parker." As soon as she blurted out the F word she regretted it. *Maybe he didn't hear me.*

"Hey, Sophie's friend Parker. How's it going?" Nick said.

He would have to repeat it, wouldn't he?

Nick extended his hand. Parker gave it a firm shake, holding eye contact with Nick for a minute before glancing at her, one eyebrow cocked.

Sophie wanted nothing more than for Nick to leave them alone but she didn't want to be rude. "Looks like you guys are slammed. What's good tonight?"

"You know it's all good." His voice dripped sex appeal, and Sophie wished he would disappear. "If you're having trouble deciding, try the shrimp pasta. Or the Southwest burger. The guacamole's full of cilantro, just the way you like it."

"Thanks." She tried to give him a you-can-go-now smile, but he seemed to misread it because he winked at her instead of leaving. *Oh God, please go.*

"We really are pretty slammed. I better get back to the kitchen. Nice to meet you, Parker. Enjoy your dinner." He bent and kissed Sophie on the side of her head then waved as he headed back across the room.

Maybe Parker didn't notice. She dared to look up and found him staring at her with a look she couldn't decipher on his face.

"Still think you're not popular?"

Sophie looked down, letting her hair cover her face to give her a second while she composed herself. "I just know all the local foodies."

Parker smiled at her. "Okay, food expert. You tell me then. What should I have for dinner? I'll take your recommendation over Nick's."

He reached for her hand again, and she relaxed as she slipped her fingers into his. "The steak tips with Portobello mushrooms is probably my favorite thing on the menu. Or the stuffed chicken breast. It's full of garlic-herb cheese. So good."

Parker had a hard time thinking about food while Sophie's fingers moved against his. When he'd heard her introduce him as her friend, he'd had a second where he thought maybe he'd been misreading the signals. But her hands seemed to be making it pretty clear that she had more-than-friendly feelings.

At least he hoped that's what she was saying. It was certainly what he was hearing. Every stroke against his palm sent a message straight to his groin, which was feeling tighter by the minute.

Laura returned to take their order, and Parker noticed the frown that flickered across her face as she eyed his hand on

Sophie's. Ever so slightly tightening his grip, he felt a ripple of pleasure as Sophie's fingers curled against his. *Good.*

Sophie ordered the steak tips, and Parker seconded. Garlic herb chicken didn't sound like a good precursor to the kissing he hoped would round out their evening.

Chapter Ten

Laughing and talking through dinner, Parker couldn't remember a time when he'd felt more at ease. The tension of the early part of their date had completely faded. When the band began playing "Wonderful Tonight" Parker gathered his nerve. "Wanna dance?"

The slow smile that pulled at Sophie's sweet lips made his stomach quake. Leading her onto the small dance floor, he slipped his arm around her waist. Her delicate hands reached up to rest on his shoulders. She kept her head lowered, seeming shy, until they started to sway to the music. He brushed his thumb back and forth over the curve of her hip, loving that he got to have his hands on her.

Drawing her closer, he was overjoyed when she inched her fingers back behind his head and lightly stroked the skin at his hairline. His entire body tingled from her touch.

Her hips shifted, curving in toward his, and he was certain she could feel how hard he was. *She's not pulling away.* The realization filled him with hope. Lowering his forehead to hers, he closed his eyes, wishing he could suspend that moment in time. Just the two of them. Moving together. Bodies touching. He hadn't realized how much he'd missed human contact and, now that he had it, he felt as if he couldn't get enough.

The final notes of the song played, and the crowd clapped. Parker brushed his nose against Sophie's and gave her a soft kiss. She kissed back, opening her mouth and licking at his lower lip. The quick brush of her tongue was enough to make his knees weak. "You want to get out of here?" he asked.

Sophie answered by taking his hand and tugging him back toward their table. *Thank God.*

The jingle of the keys in Sophie's hand as she unlocked her front door made her acutely aware of how nervous she felt. Not bad nervous. Excited. Parker followed her into the house, hands tucked in his pockets.

Sophie kicked off her heels, hoping Parker would do the same. She wanted a sign that he planned to stick around for a while. When he didn't, she moved to plan B. "You want a beer?"

"Sure."

He followed her into the kitchen. She grabbed two bottles from the top shelf and turned to see Parker watching her. His gaze swept up the length of her body to her eyes then seemed to settle on her lips. Sophie swallowed hard, her pulse picking up speed. Knocking the fridge door shut with her hip, she handed Parker a bottle. He twisted off the lid and handed the open one back to her, taking the other for himself.

She took a sip, trying to quiet the heat that seemed to be spreading throughout her body. *Calm down.* The tiny bit of liquid did little to settle her nerves but it did make her aware that she needed to pee. "I'll be right back." She set down her beer and tried to be as nonchalant as possible as she made her way to the bathroom.

As soon as she closed the door, she started to freak out. *What's wrong with me?* Her hands shook as she lifted the toilet lid and sat.

She already knew the answer. She hadn't had sex in two months. Not since the date she'd had with Bryan, Cindy's boyfriend's brother. And that had been a disaster. She'd done it mainly to prove that she was divorced and free to fuck whomever she wanted. The only problem was she hadn't really wanted to fuck him. And by the time she'd realized, she was already doing it.

This is different. Totally different. She'd known Parker forever. Had wanted him forever. None of which was making her any less nervous.

She shook her hands, trying to stop them from tingling, and then plunged them under the cold water in the sink. Focusing on her breathing as she lathered and rinsed, she studied her reflection. Her cheeks appeared to be permanently flushed. Her eyes looked wide and wild. *Jesus. I look like a lunatic. I hope I don't scare him off.*

She dried her hands then straightened her blouse, reaching into her bra cups to lift her boobs a bit higher. Taking a deep breath, she headed back to the kitchen.

Parker leaned against the kitchen counter, his long legs angled out, hips resting against her silverware drawer. His hair swept low over his eyes as he looked down, fiddling with the label on his beer bottle. He straightened as soon as he saw her.

"Hey." His voice sounded husky, and she couldn't help but wonder if he was nervous too. Though she couldn't imagine why he would be. She'd been sending him positive signals all night, and he seemed to have been picking up on them.

"Hi." She stopped as close to him as she could get without actually throwing herself at him. Leaning past him to grab her beer, she felt his hand slip around her waist. The gentle pressure of his fingers sent a rush of liquid heat to her belly, flooding her with warmth.

He stroked her hair, his fingers combing it back behind her ear before he lowered his lips to hers.

Oh God, yes. She inched closer to him, her body leaning into his. Her mouth opened, inviting his tongue inside with teasing licks. Parker responded by holding her tighter, his hand fisting her shirt.

Touch me. She wanted to feel his hands on her bare skin. His mouth was doing decadent things to hers. Dizzying, breathtaking things that made it impossible for her to focus on anything more than kissing him back.

Sliding his lips to her neck, he sucked on the tender skin just below her ear. She rocked her hips toward his, feeling him hard against her. As he pressed into her, visions flashed through her mind. Clothes coming off, strong arms carrying her to bed, Parker easing himself inside her.

She skimmed the ridges of his muscled back. *God his body is beautiful.* She explored every contour, keeping her touch light. He shuddered, and she hoped it was in response to the same exhilarating feelings that were making her shiver. Feeling bolder, she ran her fingers over his broad shoulder and smoothed her way down the plane of his chest. *So solid.* Her hand passed lower, grazing his stomach, aching to palm the bulge that had been nestled against her. Spinning with thoughts of wrapping her fingers around him, she almost didn't realize that he'd pulled back.

Parker's forehead pressed against hers, and she was just about to ask if he wanted to go to her room when he spoke. "I should go."

The words didn't compute. "Wh—"

Before she could finish he stepped away, his hands tucking themselves back into his pockets as he headed for the door.

"You don't...I mean we..." She was too stunned to get out a complete sentence. *This can't be happening.*

"I had a great time. I just...I need to go." He opened the door and stepped out into the darkness, leaving Sophie alone.

Realizing her mouth was hanging open, she closed it, trying to choke down the lump that had formed in her throat. *He just left.*

Even watching his car pull out of her driveway, she couldn't believe he was gone. *But I. We.* She could still feel his hands on her, still taste his lips. *I thought.* Tears stung the back of her eyes and rolled silently down her cheeks.

I'm such an idiot. He wasn't feeling what I was. He didn't even want to keep kissing me. The words "he's just not that into you" tumbled through her head so fast she thought she might throw up.

Wiping her hands beneath her eyes, she poured the two open beers into the sink, listening to the fizzling sound as the bubbles swirled down the drain. She tossed the empty bottles into the recycling bin under the counter and headed to her room.

The sight of the candles on her bedside table made her stomach turn. She'd put them there in hopes of setting a perfect romantic mood if they'd wound up there tonight. What a joke. He didn't want romance. Her heart sank further as the truth hit her. *He didn't want me.*

Tears slipped from her eyes once more as she stripped off the top and skirt that clearly hadn't made her look sexy enough. *Maybe Nate was right.* "Sorry, Sophie. I needed more." The pit in her stomach grew so big she thought it might consume her. *I'm not enough for anyone.*

Fumbling through her dresser, she found her favorite black yoga pants and her softest camisole and slipped them on, seeking any comfort she could possibly find. Disappointment overwhelmed her. *I can't believe I was so totally wrong.*

Parker slammed the back door of his house so hard the window rattled in its frame. Not even bothering to turn on the lights, he tossed his keys onto the kitchen counter. *Fuck.* His head pounded. *You're such a fucking dick.* Anger and frustration welled inside him, bursting out in an aggravated growl.

Every inch of him felt tense, from his shoulders to the erection that ached inside his jeans. He unzipped and began stroking with a firm grip, trying to clear his mind, concentrating only on the sensation. Intense friction combined with deep need, and within moments he felt himself giving in. Cupping his free hand, he came hard and fast into his palm, grunting with the release. His breath rasped, his abs clenching as his hips bucked forward. *Jesus.*

His heart pounded as he made his way to the bathroom. He nudged the faucet on, rinsing then lathering his hands. *Fuck.* He could still see the look on Sophie's face as he left her standing there. So hurt and confused. *How could she not be? I'm an asshole.*

Parker dried his hands and zipped up. Raking his hands through his hair, he felt as though his head might explode. *Don't just stand here alone in the dark, go talk to her. Apologize for being a dick. Tell her the truth.*

His stomach turned over at the thought. Not wanting to tell her was what had made him flee like a goddamn coward in the first place. Walking to the kitchen window, he scanned Sophie's house. The backyard was dark, but he could see a light glowing from the kitchen window. *She's still up. I'm probably the last person she wants to talk to, but she's still up.*

Stepping out into the night air, Parker's legs felt heavy. *Things can't get worse than they are right now. Just talk to her.*

He knocked on the back door. Nothing. He could see a light glowing from farther down the hallway. Scratching the back of his neck and inhaling deeply, he knocked louder. *Please come to the door.*

A shadow appeared in the corridor, and he held his breath as he saw her peek around the corner. She padded toward the door, barefoot. Parker stepped inside as soon as she opened up, afraid that if he gave her more time to consider, she'd slam it in his face.

Standing before him, arms wrapped tightly around herself, she looked so sad it broke his heart. He wanted nothing more than to turn back time to an hour before. To go back to kissing her in the kitchen with her warm body pressed against his. The makeup had been scrubbed off her face but she looked even more beautiful to him than she had on their date.

"Can we talk?"

She shrugged and stepped aside. "If you want."

I want you. He wished he could lead with those words but he knew they had more to discuss than that.

Sophie closed the door and leaned against it, arms hugging herself again. Now that she was facing him, the light reflected off her eyes—eyes rimmed in red. *Fuck. She's been crying.*

"I'm sorry, Soph."

She ducked her head, shaking it from side to side. Her hair swept back and forth in front of her so Parker couldn't even see her face. "No, I'm sorry. I misread. I shouldn't have, I didn't mean—"

"Misread what?"

"I thought... Never mind. Look, let's just forget it, okay? I mean I get it. You don't think of me that way. It's fine. I'm not exactly relationship material."

His desire to touch her was so strong his arms hurt. "Don't think of you that way? Sophie, I can't think of you any other way. I didn't leave because I'm not attracted you. I left because if I stayed I thought we might have..."

"And you didn't want to. Jesus, Parker, please don't apologize for not wanting to have sex with me."

"Not wanting…" Parker's heart beat so loudly he could barely hear his own thoughts. "I want to have sex with you more than I've ever wanted anything."

Sophie's gaze darted up and she stared at him, her eyes filled with confusion. Her lovely features were pained and clouded. She shook her head again. "But you left."

"I didn't leave because of you. I left because of me."

"It's not you it's me? Really? Tell me you didn't just say that."

Christ. Parker scrubbed his hand through his hair. *Tell her.* "I didn't mean it that way. I just…"

"Just what?" Her exasperation was evident.

Tell. Her. Bracing himself, he swallowed and looked straight into her dark eyes. *Say it.* "I've never done this before."

Her brows pinched together, furrowing her forehead. "Done what? Pity sex? Because I don't need—"

"What are you talking about?"

"This." She waved her hand back and forth between them. "Us. I'm just a friend you felt sorry for, and you couldn't go through with it. I told you, I get it."

What? No. Shit. "Sophie, I've never had sex."

Watching her mouth drop open, he seriously wished the ground would open up beneath him and swallow him whole. His cheeks burned. His jaw ached. *She thinks I'm a total loser.*

Snorting she shook her head again. "Christ, Parker. You don't have to lie. I'm a big girl. I can handle not being wanted."

Parker stared at her. Of all the reactions he'd imagined, it had never occurred to him that she wouldn't believe him. "I'm not lying. Trust me, if I was going to lie, I'd make up something way better than being a goddamn virgin."

"Will you stop saying that? Are you forgetting that we went to high school together? Chrissie told anyone who would listen how great your fucking sex life was. She actually announced it at Suzie Thomas's pre-prom party."

"Wait, what?" Parker remained dumbfounded.

"We were all doing our makeup, and CarolAnn asked who was planning on having sex that night. Chrissie said she hadn't been able to wait for prom. You guys had been at it for months already."

"Fuck." Parker paced toward the counter then turned and stared at Sophie. She looked hurt and defiant, arms still crossed in front of her. "Are you serious?"

"Yes. I remember it with crystal clarity. I was so depressed I actually slept with Donny Dugan."

Parker felt his eyes bug. "You did?"

"Yes."

"I thought you didn't even like him."

The defiance left her, and her shoulders slumped as she sank into one of the kitchen chairs. Her hands covered her eyes. "I didn't."

Seeing her with her elbows digging into her thighs and her face buried in her hands, he wanted nothing more than to hug her. Knowing that wasn't an option, he stepped closer and knelt in front of her. "Why'd you sleep with him?"

"I'd been waiting for you, okay? Is that what you wanted to hear? Once Chrissie spilled about how great you two were together, I accepted the fact that that was never going to happen so I decided to just get it over with. He was more than willing to help me out."

"I'll bet." The idea of Donny with his hands on Sophie made Parker physically ill, but the thought that she'd been waiting for him was what really threw him. "What do you mean waiting for me?"

"I'd had a crush on you since the third grade. I'd always thought... Hoped." She groaned as she sank her fingers into her hair, kneading her forehead. "It was stupid."

"Not stupid." Parker sat back on his heels. She looked so vulnerable he nearly forgot how foolish he felt. He just wanted to make her believe him. "I'm so sorry, Soph. I'm sorry Chrissie lied. I didn't know that."

Sophie slid her hands through her hair and raised her eyes enough to look at him. On his knees they were almost eye level with each other. "She really made that up?"

"Don't feel bad. She lied about a lot of shit. Believe me, I know. Now."

"So you and she, really never..."

Parker shook his head, forcing himself to keep eye contact even though he wanted to stare at the floor. Shame washed over him again.

"So when she got pregnant that was..."

Parker nodded. "She made me wait four years and then she fucked some guy she'd been seeing behind my back for one lousy month."

"And you've never...with anyone..."

"Not a lot of hot chicks in rehab." He tried to laugh, but it came out like a simple gust of breath.

The expression in her eyes changed to one he couldn't read. *Sympathy? Desire?* He was too overwhelmed to even hazard a guess.

Her hands slid down her thighs to rest on her knees. "And you wanted to? Tonight? With me?"

Parker's heart beat so irregularly, it occurred to him it might just stop altogether. "Of course. How could you even question that? Sophie, I'm crazy about you."

A smile tugged at her rosy lips. She reached toward him, and he seriously thought she might pat him on the head and send him on his way. Instead she sank her fingers into his hair, her thumb rubbing against his cheek. "Really?"

"I've got a lot of flaws, but I promise I'll never lie to you."

That promise washed away the last of her hesitation. "I'll never lie to you either," Sophie said, feeling her heartbeat throughout her body.

Parker placed his hands on the chair on either side of her legs, bracing himself, his face inches from hers. Watching as his eyes darted up and down from her eyes to her lips and back, Sophie realized he was waiting for a sign that it was okay to kiss her.

Tilting her head, she leaned toward him, stopping a breath away from making contact. Time became liquid, flowing around them as the seconds ticked by. *Kiss me. Please kiss me again.* Then his lips were on hers. A soft, gentle kiss. Tentative. It was all she needed.

Sophie wrapped her arms around Parker's neck, pulling him tightly against her. Deepening the kiss, feeling his hunger as his tongue moved against hers, Sophie relaxed. *It wasn't my imagination. It was real.* Lifting her legs, she locked them behind his back. Strong arms pulled her to the edge of the chair, pressing her against him. His hand roamed up and down her back, igniting a trail of fire that sizzled across every inch of her skin.

She tugged her mouth away from his just long enough to whisper. "Do you want to go to my room?"

It sounded funny. It was the same question she'd asked him dozens of times throughout their friendship. Only this time it meant more.

Parker wrapped his arm around her back and pushed up into a standing position, taking her with him.

Sophie gasped at the ease with which he lifted her off the chair. Clasping her legs tighter around him, she kissed him again.

Parker headed toward the front hall, but Sophie stopped him, reaching out to grab the side of the doorway. "Wait."

Freezing in his tracks, Parker drew his face away from hers. "If you don't..."

She put a finger to his lips. "My room's down here now. I didn't want to be in my old room, and my parents' room seemed wrong, so I'm over there." She nodded to what used to be her mom's sewing room.

Parker carried her down the hall, and Sophie nuzzled his neck. He smelled warm and earthy with a faint citrusy scent. She breathed him in as deeply as she could. As he lowered her onto the bed, a look of uncertainty crossed his beautiful features. She urged him forward with a gentle tug, and he crawled into bed alongside her.

Warm breath caressed the tender skin below her ear. A soft moan escaped her, instantly answered by Parker's deep, throaty sigh. Rolling her toward him, he ran his hand down her spine, curving around her ass and drawing her closer. Sophie hitched her leg over his hip, wanting to feel him. Needing to feel him. The hardness that pressed against her made her moan again.

Moving together, his lips dancing over her skin, his hands stroking her back, hips grinding into hers, she wondered if she might come just like this. Just from being so close to him. She'd never experienced such an overwhelming need. Had no idea it was possible to be this aroused from such minimal contact. *Holy shit.*

Chapter Eleven

Parker could barely believe what was happening as he slid Sophie's top over her head. Insistent fingers plucked at his shirt, and he hesitated. His scars were still not something he was comfortable with having people see. But Sophie's lips did a good job of convincing him as they licked and nipped at his while her hands pushed his shirt upward.

Realizing his shirt inevitably had to go, Parker tugged it off and tossed it aside, then quickly attempted to take Sophie back in his arms. She held back. Even in the dimly lit room, he could see her gaze trailing down his arm, across his chest, tracking the road map of scars that marred his body.

"Sorry," he said, trying to stop the images that flashed through his mind. Doctors, nurses, aides, wincing when they'd looked at him in the months after his accident.

"Sorry for what?" Sophie's eyes met his. She reached out to touch the most prominent mark on his right shoulder.

He sucked in a breath, flinching as her fingers made contact.

Her hand stilled. "Do they still hurt?"

"No, they're just not the nicest things to look at." *Understatement of the century.*

Sophie traced her fingers from one to the other, shrugging. "I kinda like them."

Parker snorted. "Why?"

Leaning forward, her hair brushing gently against his chest, she placed a whisper-soft kiss on the darkest scar. Her warm voice breathed against his skin as her lips passed over him. "They remind me that you're still alive."

Her words struck a chord deep within him. He watched in awe as she moved from one scar to the next, her nose gently grazing his chest as she kissed every mark.

Threading his fingers into her hair, he tilted her head. Eyes dark and earnest. Lips slightly parted. She was the most beautiful he'd ever seen her. Had ever seen anyone. *Sophie.* He struggled to find a single word other than her name but nothing came to mind.

Reluctant to close his eyes, he let them drift shut as his mouth found hers. Slow, gentle kisses grew more potent as their tongues met, swirling together in a delicious spiral. Bracing his arm against her back, he lowered them both onto her bed.

So soft. Everything about her was so soft. So imminently touchable. Silky hair. Velvety skin. Every curve of her body yielded to his as they rocked against each other.

Sophie deepened the kiss, sucking his tongue into her mouth as she stroked his back. *Jesus.* The touch of her hand made him crave more. He hadn't let himself think about quite how much he'd missed the feel of another person. The scent of someone else's skin.

As much as he wanted to ravish her, he forced himself to go slowly, savoring every sensation. The sweet scent rising off her body made him crazy. Kissing his way down to her collarbone, the fragrance intensified. Warm but slightly spicy, like tea with honey. His lips skimmed along the hollow of her neck. Her sighs of pleasure encouraged him as he kissed lower, tracing his fingertips beneath the cups of her bra.

Feeling her nipple pucker below the thin fabric, he kissed his way over one stiff peak, exhaling hot breath. Sophie moaned, curling her hips tighter into his. Reaching behind her, saying a silent prayer, he squeezed the clasp of her bra, breathing a sigh of relief when he felt it spring undone.

Gently slipping the strap off her shoulder, he pulled back enough to allow the rest of the bra to fall forward. The sight of Sophie's pert, pale breasts made his breath catch in his throat. Dark pink nipples, firm as gumdrops, close enough to touch. He slid one hand along her ribs, inching higher, grazing beneath each mound before passing his fingertips across the puckered flesh. A whimper escaped her as he lowered his mouth and flicked his tongue against the taut skin.

Parker shivered with need. He wanted her. Not just her lips and her breasts. Not her hands. All of her. Easing lower, he hooked his fingers into the waistband of her yoga pants. Her sexy, black, I-can't-see-straight-when-she's-wearing-them yoga pants. Hesitating to make sure she was okay, he felt her shimmy her hips as her hand joined his and tugged the pants down. *Thank God.*

Smoothing his hand across her hips, he couldn't believe how much heat radiated off her. Sophie resumed stroking his back, but only for a moment. Fingers quickly slithered around his waist and down to the button of his jeans. With one flick it popped open, and he felt her lowering the zipper.

Feeling her tug to get his jeans off was all the incentive he needed. He rolled onto his back, raised his hips and quickly rid himself of his pants. Before he could turn back toward her, Sophie's hands were on him, tracing over his chest, dancing lower, twirling through the hair on his stomach, sending goose bumps across his skin. Even through the fabric of his boxer briefs, her touch drove him wild. Drawing her palm down the length of his erection, she curved her fingers around his balls, squeezing lightly.

Tremors raced up his spine as his stomach muscles clenched. Sophie slid her hand back up then dipped beneath the fabric that separated them. Her warm fingertips against his swollen flesh were almost too much to bear. Sucking in a deep breath, he steeled himself against the pleasure. *Not now. Not yet.*

Focusing the best he could, he rolled toward her, continuing to explore her body. He teased the silky skin below her hipbone. His heart fluttered as he felt her lifting her hips toward him. As he eased her panties down her legs, his erection thickened in her hand. *Holy hell.* Breathing through his nose, he willed himself to relax. The intoxicating scent of her arousal did nothing to calm him.

Sophie's legs rubbed against his, smooth and seductive. He imagined them wrapped around his back, pulling him closer. He nearly lost track of what he was doing. *Touch her. She's real and she's right here.* How many times had he imagined this? Wished he were right where he was? Longed to run his hands across her? To feel her stroke against his skin? More than he could count or remember.

Sliding his hand back up the length of her leg, he forced himself to go as slowly as possible. Sophie appeared to be holding her breath. *She seems as nervous as I am.* The thought both soothed and scared him. He didn't want her to be nervous nor did he want to get anything wrong.

Needing to taste her again, he returned his mouth to hers. Having her lips against him brought everything back into focus. Her tongue spiraled against his, urging him on. The silky skin of her thigh curved enticingly as he reached the apex. Inching higher, his fingertips brushed against the tender folds between her legs. Velvety-smooth skin, softer than anything he could ever recall touching, greeted him, luring him nearer.

Not wanting to do anything she didn't want him to, he paused, his fingers poised. Sophie kissed him more ardently, nipping at his lower lip as her hand moved to his, pressing him against her warmth, dragging his fingers back and forth as she rocked her hips toward him. She circled against him, then let go of his hand.

Feeling her wetness was all Parker needed. He slipped his fingers between the layers, up one side, down the other, dipping inside her, twisting to slowly explore her.

"Good?" he whispered.

"Better than good." She pressed on his hand, directing his thumb to move in a tight circle as he eased a second finger inside her. She let go and wrapped her hand around his length again. He could feel her excitement heightening. Every gasp. Every sigh. Every shudder. He read each sign, gauging her response. Weighing each reaction. *Jesus. She's so responsive.*

When she tensed, her hand no longer able to continue stroking him, he knew she must be close to coming. Her breath came fast against his lips then stopped, caught in her chest as she trembled beneath him.

Making sure not to lose the rhythm of his fingers, he slid his mouth to her ear. "Breathe," he whispered.

Sophie drew in a deep breath, and Parker felt her give way. With a tremendous shudder, she contracted around his fingers, her body jolting as she cried out. *Christ.* Fascinated, Parker took it all in. The thin sheen of sweat that had bloomed across her skin, the grip of her fingers on his shoulder, the pitch of her cry, the pull, the mind-blowingly hard pull of her muscles on his fingers. He didn't know women could come like that. So hard. So intense.

"You okay?" he asked.

She nodded, her hair brushing against his chest like the caress of a summer breeze. Easing his fingers out of her, he marveled over every texture, each ridge, each swell. He tugged her toward him, wanting to hold her as close as possible. Needing to breathe in everything about her.

"Parker," she said, her voice breathy and raspy against his cheek, "I want you inside me. Make love to me."

Parker's heart beat a fierce rhythm then nearly stopped. "I don't have...I didn't bring..."

"It's okay, I'm on the Pill."

It took a moment for the words to sink in. They didn't need a condom. They were going make love. Now.

Chapter Twelve

Parker was vaguely aware of the sensation of the bed sheets against his legs as Sophie tugged them down and scooted back against the pillows. Holding himself above her, arms braced against the mattress, erection pressed against her stomach, he couldn't get over how small she seemed. How fragile. Not wanting to crush her, he held himself as steady as possible with the cushiony pillow top giving beneath his hands.

Sophie trailed her toes up his calf, sending the sweetest thrill straight up his leg to his balls. Wetness streaked across her belly as he slid back and forth. *Is she ready?*

As if she heard his question she reached between them, curling her fingers around him, guiding him lower. Her hips shifted as she wiggled until he felt himself flush against her. Heat. Surreal heat seemed to be beckoning him.

Digging his knees into the bed, Parker tilted his hips forward, moving as slowly as he could manage. The tip of his erection nuzzled against her, slipping between her folds. *I'm inside her.* The thought struck him. *Inside Sophie.*

Pivoting below him, Sophie wrapped her legs around him, drawing him farther in. *Jesus.* Surrounded by warmth, he found it impossible to concentrate on anything other than the feel of her body. *This is really happening.*

Soft lips grazed his neck, licking and nipping, jolting him from his mind into the present. Nervousness faded, replaced by intense need—the need to move inside her, to feel her body moving against his, to kiss her.

Finding her mouth, he licked at her sweetness, feeling her lips spring open beneath his. Her tongue met his, eager, teasing. Her rich taste mesmerized him as he breathed her in. His head swam with the mix of sensations—her breasts rubbing against his chest, her hips grinding against his on every downward thrust, her fingers fisting his hair, each tug sending shivers down his back. *Oh God.*

Pressure built inside him, filling him. Everything felt heavy. His chest. His balls. Tension coiled deep within his stomach, spiraling lower. Sophie rocked with him, lifting her hips to meet each stroke in and out of her body. *So wet. So good.* As much as he wanted the moment to last, he couldn't hold back any longer.

Burrowing his face against her neck, breathing in great puffing gasps, he let go. The orgasm burst from him, sending his hips hard into Sophie's. Wave upon wave of tension released as he pulsated inside her, trying to stifle his groans.

Shaking, drained, lightheaded, he slowly became aware of Sophie's hand stroking his back.

With his breath still rasping, he kissed his way up the arch of her throat and along her jaw until his lips met hers. Even their kiss felt different now. Less urgent but more intimate.

His tongue grazed hers, slow and sweet, as their bodies continued to rock together. *I'm still inside her.* The realization filled him with happiness that continued even as he slipped out of her. She curled toward him, her arm snug around his chest. Leaning closer, he kissed her again, savoring the moment. Then it hit him. *She didn't come.*

Sophie slid her fingers into Parker's hair, loving the silkiness and trying to remember the last time she'd felt so content.

"Are you okay?" he asked, his lips a whisper from hers.

85

She nodded and kissed him again, loving that she now felt free to do that. To kiss him any time she felt like.

Parker pulled back, brushing her hair out of her eyes. "You didn't...just now. Did you?"

It took her a second to realize what he was asking. "Oh. No." Heat crept into her cheeks.

"Sorry." The downward cast of his eyes surprised her.

"Don't be sorry. I never do. I mean not, you know, during." *Oh God, he's going to think there's something wrong with me.*

Parker's hand traced up and down her back, creating a tingling so strong she nearly forgot what they were discussing. "Never?" he asked.

Heat burned even more intensely in her cheeks. She shook her head.

"But you did before."

"Oh yeah." Just the memory of it was enough to make her internal muscles flutter.

Parker trailed his hand over her hip, taking the tingling along with it. "So we could do that again."

Before Sophie could answer, his fingers slipped between her legs. Sucking in a gulp of air she nodded. *Jesus, where did he learn how to do that?* His fingers moved over her so slowly, bringing every nerve ending to life. Her hips jerked forward as he hit just the right spot.

"Good?" he asked, kissing beneath her ear.

"Uh-huh." A small groan escaped as he licked her earlobe, his hand continuing to work its magic.

Parker trailed kisses from her forehead down her nose before settling in on her mouth. His tongue slipped between her lips in sync with his fingers. Sophie shivered, straining toward him. She could feel him hard against her hip, rocking in rhythm. Knowing he was so turned on made her even more excited. Pressure built deep in her belly as heat spread lower. *God, yes.*

As if he knew exactly what she was thinking, Parker slowed his movements, drawing out the pleasure until she could no longer keep from quivering. Tongue, thumb, hips—everything spiraled against her until she could scarcely breathe. A high-pitched cry escaped her as she clenched a handful of bed sheets. Hips bucking forward, she came hard and fast, moaning into his mouth.

She broke the kiss, her head thrashing against the pillow as the aftershocks jolted through her. When she could finally open her eyes, she found Parker staring right at her with a look she couldn't discern on his face.

"What?" She breathed the word, still unable to catch her breath.

"You're so fucking beautiful."

She raked a hand through the tangled mass of her hair, laughing. As she tried to force herself to breathe, she inhaled deeply, surprised when she let out a huge hiccup. Sophie clapped her hand over her mouth but a second, louder hiccup escaped. "Shit."

Parker shook with laughter. "I can't believe you still get hiccups."

"I don't." She hiccupped again. "I haven't had them in ages."

"Likely story. You got them after practically every test in school."

"I know. I always thought they were brought on by stress release." *Hiccup. Dammit.*

"Well, I don't know of a better stress releaser than an orgasm."

The grin on Parker's face made him look completely irresistible. She wanted to kiss him, but as soon as she got her face close enough to his, a hiccup interrupted. Groaning, she fell back against the bed and pulled a pillow over her head.

"Do you have any peanut butter?" Parker asked.

"You want a sandwich?"

Laughter tumbled out of him again, vibrating the bed. "No. Do you have any or not?"

"Of course I have peanut butter."

"Come on." He tugged at her hand.

Sophie hiccupped and lifted the pillow enough to peer out at him. "Where are we going?"

"We need peanut butter."

Parker pulled on his boxers and watched as Sophie slipped his T-shirt over her head. Seeing her in his clothes sent a rush through him that made him want to forget about the damned peanut butter and toss her back on the bed, but the next hiccup reminded him of the matter at hand.

She reached for her panties but he stopped her. "I assume we're only going to the kitchen. I think you're dressed enough."

Sophie smirked at him, igniting another burst of heat that coursed through him. He linked his fingers with hers as they walked down the hall. He loved that she had to go up on her toes to reach the peanut butter off the top pantry shelf.

"Now what?" she asked, handing him the jar.

He unscrewed the lid, surprised to find the protective seal still in place. "An unopened jar of peanut butter? Cut down on your habit, have you?"

"No, I finished a jar with breakfast." A loud hiccup punctuated her indignation.

Parker snorted, peeling the Mylar cover off the jar. "Spoon, please."

"Maybe later, right now I just want to know what the peanut butter's for."

Smartass. He dipped the spoon into the jar, giving a quick stir before scooping up a heaping amount. "Open wide."

Hiccup. "What?"

"You heard me. Open up." He held the spoonful in front of her mouth. "One big mouthful. No dainty licks."

"Are you kidding me?" *Hiccup.*

"Do you want to get rid of your hiccups?"

She nodded, her breasts giggling beneath his shirt as another hiccup shook through her.

"Trust me." He tried to keep eye contact but couldn't help glancing at her mouth as her lips parted and then closed around the spoon. His entire body reacted, tensing in a torturously pleasant way as he withdrew the utensil. "Chew then swallow."

Parker watched as she managed the mouthful. She was clearly struggling as she tried not to laugh, but Parker was the one who could barely swallow. His mouth had grown dry. His throat felt tight. He wondered how he was going to watch her for another second and not kiss her. He tossed the spoon into the sink, trying to distract himself.

Sophie finally gulped. "I can't believe you made me eat that much peanut butter."

"Are your hiccups gone?"

They both listened.

"Holy shit," she said, putting her hand on her chest as if she was waiting to feel another outburst. "I think they are."

"You're welcome." Parker took a bow.

"That's insane. All these years I've suffered with hiccups for hours at a time and all I needed to do was eat peanut butter?"

"I know, right? Best trick I learned in rehab. Trust me, hiccups and recovery from surgery do not mix. One of the nurses there taught me the peanut butter cure."

"She's a genius."

"Yep. Best cure ever. And tasty too." He leaned in and kissed her, moaning at the salty sweetness of her lips.

"There's plenty more, you know." Sophie pulled away and reached for the jar. She swirled her index finger in the jar then held it in front of Parker. Mischief sparkled in her eyes.

Jesus, Sophie, could you be any sexier? He held her gaze as he swooped his tongue around her finger before sucking it into his mouth. The tiny gasp that escaped her made every muscle in his torso contract. She withdrew her finger slowly, running it over his lower lip before she pulled it away. Without another thought, Parker's mouth was back on hers.

Sophie's tongue mingled with his, as her hand sank into his hair. He held her tight, feeling his erection swell against her. "What do you say we go back to your room?"

"I say that's an even better idea than the peanut butter."

Sophie could never remember her bed feeling more comfortable than it did with Parker lying beside her. Parker smiled, still staring at her with the same intent expression. Taking her hand he linked his fingers with hers, pressing them into the pillow. "So fucking beautiful." And his lips were back on hers. Soft. Gentle. Making Sophie feel as if she were melting right into the mattress.

He eased himself on top of her, sliding against her. *Oh, God. So hard. So good.* How could he possibly feel so good rubbing against her? Spreading her legs with his knees, he slipped easily between them. With a tilt of her pelvis, he pushed inside her.

"Parker," she whispered his name.

"Mmm," he answered, sliding his lips to her throat, nibbling at her neck, her collarbone, sending her body soaring once again.

She tightened her grip on his hand as they moved together. Her other hand burrowed into his silky hair. The mix of sensations was too much. The grasp of his hand on hers, the softness of his hair, his firm chest grazing hers, his warm breath at her shoulder, his hardness rocking in and out of her.

Giving in to all of it, she brought her hips up hard against his. Parker swiveled on every downward thrust, grinding his pelvis against hers.

Oh yes. She locked her legs around him, pulling him tighter. Parker took the hint, pressing closer. Each gyration sent a jolt of pleasure through her. Nothing had ever felt like this before. This wasn't jackrabbit, in-and-out sex, this was sensual, purposeful friction. Intense. Mind-numbingly intense. And so damn sexy she could barely breathe.

Parker pulled away, and Sophie immediately missed the weight of his body. Before she could complain, he slipped his hand down the length of her torso, briefly tracing around her belly button before trailing lower and settling where their bodies were joined.

Gasping as he worked his thumb against her, she could see the same look on his face. His words echoed in her head—"so fucking beautiful". Looking up at him, seeing herself through his eyes, she felt beautiful. She felt downright ethereal. Every inch of her sang beneath him, and it was the sweetest sound she could imagine.

Once more, the pressure built within her. "Yes." The word came out before she could stop it.

A grin spread across Parker's face as he gazed at her through hooded eyes. *So sexy.* Each pass of his thumb made her muscles tighten and she felt him expand inside her in response. Concentrating as hard as she could, she focused on the sensation, constricting her muscles, letting the tension build until she couldn't stand it anymore.

Oh, God... Her neck arched against the pillow as her eyes slammed shut. Wave after wave crashed over her as she contracted around him. A low growl left Parker. The deepest, sexiest sound she'd ever heard. With a final thrust he let go, pulsing inside her.

Sophie ran her hand down his sweaty chest, feeling his heart pounding rapidly beneath her fingers. Urging him closer with her legs, she was grateful when he was once again pressed against her. Parker nuzzled her neck, and she sighed, wrapping her arms around him.

He eased himself out of Sophie and sprawled alongside her, pulling her close. He kissed her shoulder, his silky hair feathery against her still sensitized skin. "You've really never done that before?" he asked.

Laughter tumbled out of Sophie before she could stop it. Tears rolled from her eyes. Parker gaped at her. *He must think I'm crazy.*

Gulping air, she tried to speak but as soon as she opened her mouth fresh giggles poured out. "I'm sorry," she squeaked. "No, I've never. Not even close."

A mix of pride and relief filled Parker. Though for the life of him, he couldn't figure out why she was laughing. He didn't care. He loved the sound. Loved the vibration of her against him, so warm and full of life.

Running his fingers through her hair, he felt wet streaks from her tears. He brushed at them with his thumbs, trying to absorb as many details of the moment as possible. *I can't believe this is real.* Three hours earlier he was alone in his house, wrecking their evening and now...

Sophie shifted alongside him, her breast grazing his chest, her hand resting on his hip. The gesture was so simple yet so intimate Parker felt his chest tighten.

"Can I ask you something?" she said, her fingers tracing a pattern on his lower back, sending a fresh batch of tingles through him.

"Sure."

"How did you... I mean if this was your first...never mind." She closed her eyes and shook her head.

Parker smoothed her hair behind her ear. "How did I what?"

Eyes still closed she took a deep breath and blew it out slowly. "You just really seemed to know what you were doing. I've never had anyone...no one's ever..."

"I just paid attention." He trailed his hand along her jaw, tilting her chin up and kissing her.

Sophie made a tiny gasp, and Parker felt her nipple stiffen against his chest.

"See?" he said, rubbing his thumb against her other nipple. "You gave me all the clues. I just put them together."

"You put them together really well."

Parker grinned so broadly his cheeks ached. "I'm glad."

"Me too." She bit her lip. "I hope this doesn't sound stupid but I wish this was my first time. I wish you'd been my first and that it had been this amazing."

Parker's heart swelled as he held her closer. "That's probably the most awesome thing anyone's ever said to me."

"Probably? Well, I'll have to try harder next time." Sophie's lips brushed his, stopping words and thoughts as he let himself get lost in her.

Chapter Thirteen

Sunlight shone brightly against Parker's still-closed eyelids. He raised his arm to shield his eyes, squinting to look around the room. Sophie's room. A grin spread across his face as he remembered the night before but faded when he realized she was no longer in bed with him. He stretched, feeling his thigh muscle tense and nearly cramp.

Tanya's voice popped into his mind. "What the hell have you been doing?"

Chuckling, he reached over the side of the bed, plucking his boxers off the floor and slipping them on. Before he'd finished easing into his jeans, Sophie peeked around the corner of the doorway.

"Morning," she said. Her hair was pulled into a messy ponytail, long pieces loose and framing her face. The yoga pants were back on, along with a cropped hoodie that was only partway zipped, so bits of both her belly and her cleavage still showed. *Holy hell.*

"Good morning." He made his way toward her, taking in the sway of her hips as she leaned against the doorframe. Images of the night before flickered through his mind as he dipped his head to kiss her.

The small sigh that escaped her when his lips touched hers was enough to make him want to scoop her up and toss her onto the bed. Her warm fingers sank into the hair at the base of his neck, sending shivers down his spine.

"I made breakfast," she whispered. "But I have to go. I've got an appointment in twenty minutes."

Parker groaned. *Appointment.* "Shit. So do I." He kissed her again, loving how warm she felt. "Okay. Quick breakfast then."

Sophie slipped her hand into his and pulled him down the hall toward the kitchen. The table was already set, but just for one. Scrambled eggs, bacon, toast and fruit salad.

I can't believe I slept through her cooking all of this. The aroma overwhelmed him as he realized how hungry he was. "You can't stay and eat?" he asked, sitting and tugging her onto his lap.

She shook her head, the gentle back-and-forth motion surrounding him with the sweet scent of her perfume. "Nope. It's all yours."

Parker plucked a strawberry off his plate and held it in front of her. "One bite?"

"Okay, maybe just one." Her eyes twinkled as she leaned forward, taking the berry between her lips for a second before biting down.

Parker groaned, feeling himself harden beneath her.

She giggled, shifting in his lap with a playful wriggle before she stood.

"I had no idea you had such a cruel streak," he said, already missing the feel of her.

Laughing harder, she dipped her head and gave him a strawberry-flavored kiss. "Terribly cruel. Sadistic. Now eat your breakfast."

Parker plucked a strip of bacon off his plate and stuffed it in his mouth, chewing as he watched her gather her purse and briefcase. "You busy later?"

"What'd you have in mind?"

Again their night flashed through his mind. "Whatever you'd like. Movie? Pizza?"

"How about both? Here. And a swim if it doesn't rain?"

"Sounds great."

Parker finished eating, washed his plate and placed it in the cupboard, still unable to believe how much his life had changed in less than twenty-four hours. He caught himself whistling as he walked back to his house. He couldn't remember the last time he'd been in such a great mood.

His euphoria faded somewhat when he entered his house. The silence was an instant reminder that his dad wasn't there. Not that he'd necessarily have told his father what happened last night. He probably wouldn't have. Or at least not the details. But now his dad would never even know that he and Sophie were... What were they? Together? Dating? Whatever they were doing it would have made his dad happy, and the fact that he couldn't share it with him ate away a little of Parker's joy.

The phone rang before he'd even tossed his keys on the kitchen counter. The number wasn't familiar but he answered anyway.

"It's true. You're back." The deep voice was instantly recognizable. Joey.

"It's true."

"I tried you last night, but there was no answer, and it's still your dad's answering machine message, so I thought maybe my dad had it wrong about you being home."

"Nope, I'm here." *Gotta change that outgoing message.* The thought of erasing his dad's voice made Parker's stomach tense, but the house was his now. *Everything's got to change.*

"I'm sorry I missed the funeral. I had an away game. I'd have been there if I could."

"No worries. Thanks."

Joey cleared his throat, and Parker could tell he was uncomfortable. It was the same sound he'd heard all of the few times they'd spoken since the accident. "Yeah. Hey, I was calling to see what you're up to next weekend. You wanna come watch a game? I can get you seats right behind first base."

For years Parker would have done anything for those seats. Hell, he'd spent countless hours daydreaming that he'd be able to offer those seats to whomever he chose. His dad. His wife. Anyone he wanted to make feel special. Now Joey was offering them to him. "Okay. Sure. Can you make it two, though?"

"Seats? Sure? Who you bringing?"

Parker hesitated. Dates with Sophie were certainly not implied yet. For all he knew she had a wedding that night. Or wouldn't even want to go. Last thing he wanted was to look like an ass. "What, like I can't get a date?" *Maybe I can. Hopefully. Shit. Can I?*

Joey laughed. "Give it your best shot. I'll put you down for two tickets. Just go to the box office—they'll have them. Make sure you bring ID. Buddy of mine left his wallet at home, and they wouldn't let him in until halfway through the game when a security guard finally came and asked me to prove who he was."

"ID. Got it. See you then."

If things went as planned, next week he'd be hanging out with Joey and Sophie, just like the old days. Except absolutely nothing was like it was in the old days.

Sophie rushed from her meeting at the flower market to the community health club.

An impatient Cindy greeted her out front. "You're late," she said.

"I know. I got here as fast as I could. Manuel was in the mood to chitchat."

"Manuel was in the mood to stare at you in your exercise gear."

Sophie laughed. "Maybe. But we got a great deal for the Robinson wedding."

They made their way down the crowded hallway toward the exercise rooms. Cindy elbowed Sophie as they shoved their gym bags into the cubbies outside the Zumba classroom. "Stop yawning. You're making me sleepy."

"Sorry," Sophie said, unable to keep from smirking. "I didn't sleep much last night."

"I knew it. You had sex."

"A little louder please. I don't think the people in the spin class heard you."

Cindy bounced on her toes. "I don't care about them. How was it? Was it awesome? Was he awesome?"

Sophie nodded, feeling the flush spread across her cheeks. "It was amazing."

"Yes," Cindy boomed.

"Shhh." Sophie dragged her down the corridor so there was no one immediately around them. "Will you please stop yelling everything?"

"Sorry. Now tell me. I want details. Big?"

"Cindy."

"Come on, Soph. Give me something to work with here. Bigger than Nate?"

The grin returned before she could stop it. "Yes."

"Yay." Cindy clapped her hands. "And he was good?"

Sophie looked over her shoulder to make sure no one was within earshot. "It was seriously the best sex I've ever had."

"Get out," Cindy bellowed as Sophie pushed her farther down the hallway.

"Can you please be a little more discreet?"

"I'm sorry, I'm just happy for you. And a little shocked. First times aren't usually described as the best anything."

First times. That was one detail she wasn't about to share with Cindy. The fact that she'd been Parker's first was their secret and theirs alone. Her heart skipped a beat just thinking about it.

She lowered her voice to a whisper. "It wasn't just our first time together. It was the first time I ever...you know...during sex."

Cindy's eyes bugged to a comical size. "Are you kidding me?"

"Nope." Cindy had tried countless pep talks over the years, giving Sophie all sorts of tips and techniques in an attempt to help her achieve orgasms during intercourse. All to no avail. "I didn't the first time but the second time, oh my God."

"Marry him."

Sophie snorted. "I think I should probably see if he asks me out again before I plan to marry him."

"Fine. Date him a few more times. Then marry him. He's the one. I know it."

"You haven't even met him."

"I know. And I already like him so much more than I ever liked Nate. Marry him, I'm telling you."

Sophie laughed. "I love you."

Cindy studied her for a minute, eyes narrowed. "You love him, don't you?"

Flinching Sophie stepped back. "Love him? Cin, we just started seeing each other."

"After knowing each other for years and having a secret crush on him half your life. And now all of a sudden, you're having the best sex ever."

"He's just a very attentive lover."

Cindy sighed. Sophie knew she'd be able to distract her with more sex details. "How attentive?"

"Like a goddamned mind reader. I didn't know guys could be like that. It was like he didn't even care about anything other than making me feel good."

"I'm melting here."

"How do you think I felt?" The memories alone were enough to turn her insides molten.

"Pretty damn good apparently." Cindy grinned. "So, when do I get to meet this sex god? Not that I don't already adore him, but I do want a closer look."

Meet him? She hadn't thought about that. How would he feel about meeting her friends? They hadn't discussed, well, anything. Nervousness bubbled inside her. Would he even want to get to know her friends? Was this too much too soon? He was just home from rehab, still adjusting to his father's death. What if a relationship was the last thing on his mind? "I don't know. I guess I'll see how things go."

"Yeah. You do that. I'll start looking for my maid-of-honor dress."

"Cut that out."

Cindy cackled as she headed toward the Zumba room. "Come on, let's exercise. I don't want to look fat in the wedding photos."

Lafourche Parish Library

Chapter Fourteen

Parker settled himself into the cushioned massage table, letting the heated blanket on his back lull him into a state of bliss. By the time Tanya entered the room he was nearly asleep.

"How's it going?" Tanya asked.

Parker opened his eyes, looking through the cutaway area of the table. Tanya's black and gray Chucks had purple laces in them today. "Nice shoes."

"Thanks, kid." She pointed a toe, holding her foot closer to the table. "What's going on with you? We working on anything in particular today?"

"Whatever you want."

Tanya snorted as she removed the blanket. The air in the room coated his back in a cool rush. Her small but firm hands went to work, starting at his shoulders, making their way down his back. "Did you start working again?"

"Did I ever stop?"

"No, I mean, lifting shit. You doing actual landscaping? Your knots aren't in the usual pattern. You're doing something different."

Parker breathed out a laugh, glad he was facedown so she couldn't see the grin that he couldn't keep off his face. The only thing he'd lifted was Sophie, and he didn't want to spend too much time thinking about that while he was ninety-percent naked on a massage table. Tanya was cool but he still didn't want to make an ass of himself.

Knowing she wouldn't stop asking until she had an answer, he took a deep breath. "I had my date last night."

Tanya's hands froze for a second, and he could practically hear the wheels turning in her mind. "That's right. How could I forget? How'd it go?"

Parker concentrated on the pain as she dug her fingers into a particularly sore spot below his hipbone. "Great. Really great."

"Great enough that your pelvic muscles got a workout, I see." She chuckled, and he heard her getting the minty liniment that burned and chilled simultaneously.

Tensing as her hands rubbed the icy liquid on him, he exhaled long and slow. "You talk to all your clients this way?"

Tanya laughed. "Only the ones I like. So, can I assume from how happy you sound that everything went well?"

"Yes."

"Awesome. I'm glad you had a good night, kid. You certainly deserve it."

Parker had never thought about deserving a good time. Certainly not in the form of sex. And he'd never imagined that last night would work out as well as it had. "Thanks."

"You seeing her again?"

The smile returned instantly. "Tonight."

"Good boy. Don't be one of those idiot guys who makes her wait for you to call."

Parker snorted. "Yes, ma'am."

"And don't call me ma'am." She dug her fingers in extra hard, and Parker laughed as he felt the knot finally release.

The pizza box burned Parker's hand, but holding it from underneath was the only way he could manage to carry it along with a six-pack and the bouquet of bright blue hydrangeas he'd picked up on the way. *Is she going to think flowers are stupid?* He didn't have to worry too long because she answered the door two seconds after he leaned on the doorbell with his shoulder.

"Oh my God, they're beautiful." Sophie's eyes lit up as she stared at the flowers. "I can't believe you remembered that I love hydrangeas."

"I used to watch you clip them every summer. You always said there weren't enough blue flowers in the world."

For a second Sophie looked like she might cry, and he wondered if he'd said something wrong. "They're still my favorites. And there *aren't* enough blue flowers. Thanks for remembering that."

I remember everything about you. Parker followed her into the house, thankful to be able to put the pizza box down before his hand melted. He grabbed a beer, allowing the cool bottle to soothe the overheated skin on his palm. "Beer?"

"Sure, thanks."

He twisted the cap off and handed the beer to Sophie, watching as she took a sip. "How'd your meetings go today?"

Sophie took down plates and headed for the family room. "Good. What about you?"

"Not bad." He put the pizza box on the coffee table and sat next to her on the sofa.

Sophie curled her legs under her and leaned closer, the sweet smell of her surrounding him. "Just not bad?"

He kissed her. Even the light brush of her lips felt electric. "Better now," he whispered, kissing her again. Sophie's tongue met his in a gentle caress, and he thought about how cold pizza is almost as good as hot pizza.

"Mmmm. I could totally forget about things like dinner when you're around," she said.

"Was just thinking the same thing." Parker was about to kiss her again when the phone rang. Sophie startled. "You can get that, you know."

She reached for the phone on the end table, scowling when she looked at the caller ID. Without answering she stuck the phone back in the charging cradle.

"Everything okay?" Parker asked.

Sophie nodded, not looking directly at him. "It's my parents. I'll call them back."

"You could have picked up."

Her eyes darted to his, and he could see that she was chewing on her lower lip like she always used to when she was stressed. "Let's just say I don't want to ruin our evening."

"What's going on with your folks?"

Sophie inhaled deeply then sank back against the couch. "You know my divorce was a pretty messy affair, right? Lots of gossip. Not exactly quiet."

"Yeah."

She looked so stressed and vulnerable he wanted to hug her, but he just listened.

Her hand went to the base of her neck and started massaging. "Well, part of the reason they moved down to Florida ahead of schedule was to get away from me. From the 'disgrace I brought on the family' to be more precise."

The hurt in her voice made Parker's stomach twist. "Your ex is the asshole who cheated on you. What disgrace?"

"They thought I should have worked things out with him. I think they thought it was my fault that our marriage didn't work. I don't know." She shook her head, staring down into her lap as she fiddled with the hem of her shirt.

Karen Stivali

Parker reached for her hand, linking his fingers with hers and rubbing her wrist with his thumb. "That's bullshit. You know that, right?"

She half shrugged, half nodded.

"Hey, listen to me." He tilted her chin up with his free hand, waiting for her to make eye contact before he continued. "Relationships fail all the time. That's not a disgrace. And in this case, if your folks are mad at anyone, it should be your ex, not you. If that's really their attitude, then I'm glad you're not taking their calls. You don't need that kinda crap."

"Thanks for saying that."

"I'm not just saying it. I know a thing or two about what it feels like to be cheated on. It's easy to blame yourself. I know."

Sophie's eyes darkened. "Did you? Blame yourself, for Chrissie?"

It had been over two years, and Parker hadn't really talked to anyone about what he'd gone through after Chrissie cheated on him. He'd certainly had enough time to think about it on his own, though. Hour upon hour spent turning it over in his mind while his body recovered from the accident. He knew Sophie needed his honesty.

He continued to rub her wrist, letting the smooth feel of her skin soothe him. "I did for a while. Hell, I'd planned on marrying her and then—boom—she was marrying some other guy. That stung."

"I bet."

The sensation had dulled over the years, but talking about it still pained him. "After a while it's not even about the act itself—it's just about the betrayal. Maybe it's me, but as far as I'm concerned, if you care about someone, you don't do something that's going to hurt them. It would have been bad enough if she'd decided she wanted to see this other guy and

106

had broken up with me. The fact that she did it all behind my back was what hurt the most."

Sophie nodded.

"Yes. Oh my God. I totally agree. I'd have been devastated if Nate had said he wanted to end our marriage after a few months, but we could have talked about it and gone our separate ways and, in the long run, that would have hurt so much less than finding out while I was getting a haircut."

Parker's eyes bugged. "What?"

"I was in the middle of getting my hair done and I heard two women gossiping while they were getting manicures. They hadn't noticed I was sitting there and they were openly discussing what a shame it was and how 'poor Sophie probably doesn't have a clue'. They were right. I didn't.

"One of the manicurists saw me and shushed them, but I was so freaked out I left mid-haircut. Just grabbed my purse and walked out like a lunatic."

Parker squeezed her fingers tighter. "I'm sorry, Soph."

"It gets worse. I went straight to his job—hair still damp, clips on one side of my head—walked into his office and caught him. With her."

"Jesus."

Sophie snorted. "I've never been more humiliated in my life."

Parker's stomach knotted in sympathy. "You realize this makes me want to beat the living shit out of your ex, right?"

"There was a time when I'd have gladly taken you up on that offer. Now I'm just thankful it's over. I never would have been happy with him. And he never would have been happy with me."

"You deserve to be happy."

Sophie tilted her head, a rueful smile tugging at her lips. "So do you."

"I am. Now."

Chapter Fifteen

"Ready for that swim?" Parker asked when the last of the pizza had been wrapped and stuck in the fridge.

"Absolutely."

"Oh, hey, I almost forgot. Are you busy next Friday night?"

Sophie thought for a second.

Please say no.

"I don't think so," she said.

"Good. How'd you like to come with me to see Joey play?"

Sophie's eyes widened. "Seriously?"

"He called and offered me seats behind first base. You wanna go?" *Say yes.* He realized he was holding his breath.

"Sure. Sounds like fun. I wasn't sure the two of you were still friends. You've hardly mentioned him."

"To be honest, I was surprised to hear from him. He's got this thing about hospitals and medical facilities. You know, from when his mom was sick when he was a kid. I didn't see him once the whole time I was recovering."

"That sucks."

Parker shrugged. "It is what it is. It's not like I expected people to put their lives on hold waiting for me to get better."

"Still..."

"I know. We could have been better about staying in touch, but I think the blame goes both ways."

"Well, to answer your question—yes, I'd love to go." A funny look flickered across her face as she narrowed her eyes. "Did you tell him I might come with you?"

"Nope. Just asked for two tickets."

Sophie laughed, the sound sending warm tremors down Parker's spine. "Good. I can't wait to see the look on his face when he sees both of us."

Both of us. Together. "Me neither."

Sophie carried two towels over to the edge of the pool and placed them by the ladder. "I can't believe how warm it is tonight."

Parker nodded, closing his eyes and taking a deep breath. "Finally smells like summer."

The water, which had still had a chill to it days before was now a comfortable temperature. Sophie sat on the side of the pool, slowly kicking her legs back and forth, watching Parker. He walked the perimeter of the pool, reaching behind him to pull his T-shirt over his head. Air got momentarily stuck in Sophie's lungs. *God he's hot.* He threw her a quick smirk then dove straight into the pool. His body skimmed the water, long and lean, the muscles on his back rippling as he swam straight to her.

Rising out of the water right in front of her, he looked like a statue caught in the rain. Droplets ran down his chest, over the contours of his arms. He raked his hands through his hair, slicking it back off his face. A single bead ran down his perfect nose. Sophie swallowed hard.

Parker raised an eyebrow at her. "Don't tell me you've turned into one of those girls who doesn't want to get her hair wet."

Sophie snorted. "Hardly."

"You're looking awfully dry right now."

Was he always this sassy? Yes. It was part of what had made her fall for him over and over.

"You saying you want me wet?"

The grin on his face made her stomach flutter. He answered with a splash that sent water sprinkling across her thighs and belly. "Maybe."

"Hey." She kicked her leg, scattering a spray of water across his chest.

"You know it's much easier to splash from inside the pool." He slammed the heel of his hand against the surface, causing a miniature wave to land on her lap.

"I can't believe you did that."

Mischief twinkled in his eyes. "What? This?" he said, doing it again.

"You're in so much trouble now."

"Not unless you catch me." He splashed her again then took off, heading for the deep end.

Sophie slid into the pool, took a deep breath and dove underwater. She hadn't swum with her eyes open in so long it felt funny. The underwater lights made everything shimmery. She broke the surface of the water and was surprised when Parker wasn't where she'd thought he would be. Kicking her legs to stay afloat, she spun just in time to see him beside her.

"Wet. But not quite wet enough." A tidal wave engulfed her, and she momentarily went under, bobbing back up with her hair streaming down in front of her face. Knowing he was still right in front of her, she shook her head hard enough to make water spray all over his face.

"Oh, you're going down." Parker disappeared, and before Sophie could see where he went she felt him grab her legs and tug her under.

They wrestled beneath the surface, flipping over one another for all of three seconds before Parker pulled her into a kiss. Sophie forced herself to open her eyes, checking to make sure all of this was real. Parker's open eyes greeted her before closing as he kissed her harder, his arms tightening around her waist as they spiraled through the water.

Just as Sophie was about to run out of breath, he pulled her up. A rush of air swirled around them as they bobbed together. Before she even had a chance to take a full gulp of air his mouth was back on hers. His tongue, warm and sweet, worked its way into her mouth, and she locked her legs around his waist. Parker managed to keep kissing her as he kicked his way over to the shallow end of the pool.

She could tell he'd started walking but was too mesmerized by his mouth to give it much thought. Kissing had always been one of her favorite activities, but kissing Parker elevated it to a new level. She didn't want to stop. Ever.

The night air felt cool against her overheated skin as he lifted her out of the water and set her down on the edge of the pool. No longer needing to hold her, his hands were now free to explore. They moved in tandem, thumbs stroking her cheekbones as his fingers sank into her hair. He seemed so totally focused on Sophie that it took her breath away.

He kissed his way over to her ear. "God, it feels good to kiss you."

"Don't stop."

She could feel his smile against her cheek as his lips made their way back to hers. His hands ran down her arms to her hips. Strong fingers pulled her to the very edge of the pool as his torso pressed against her thighs. She was about to suggest they go inside when Parker began to kiss his way down her neck. His tongue traced a delicate pattern of swirls along the sensitive skin, and Sophie forgot what she'd been thinking about.

Massaging her hips with his fingers, he made his way lower, covering her belly with a combination of kisses and licks that had her gasping harder than she had when she'd come up for air. He reached her bikini bottoms and traced a finger beneath the top edge, a distinct question in his touch. His lips moved over the damp fabric, pressing kisses against her. Sophie moaned.

"Lay back," he whispered against her inner thigh, licking and nibbling as she felt herself lying down on the rough concrete.

Parker eased her legs over his shoulders continuing to kiss a maddening path from her thighs to her hips then lower again.

Sophie's brain tumbled around in her head. *Feels so good. But wait.* "What if someone sees us?" She lifted her head and saw Parker's eyes glittering up at her.

"The only house with a view of your backyard is mine. And I'm..." He placed a kiss on her hipbone. "Already..." A second kiss graced her belly, right above her bikini. "Here."

His lips trailed lower, only this time, instead of kissing through the fabric, he eased it out of the way, placing his mouth directly on her.

Sophie groaned as her head lay back on the ground. *Oh God.* She couldn't remember the last time she'd been kissed like this.

Parker moved slowly. Gently. Exploring. Fingers joined his tongue, spreading her open, creating more heat and tension than she knew what to do with.

A soft whimper escaped her as she arched her hips, wanting more. Needing more. Parker eased his fingers inside her, first one then two, as his tongue worked magic against her swollen flesh. *Oh please.* Her fingers sank into his hair. *So good.* He brought her to the brink twice, backing off each time with soft kisses as she regained control.

Sweet torture kept her locked in place. Her heels pressed into his back as her nails scratched across his scalp. Parker moaned, the vibration trilling straight through her. His free hand slid up her body, stroking the tender skin between her breasts as his thumb rubbed back and forth against one stiff nipple.

No longer able to keep her breaths even, she panted, whispering his name. He focused his effort, moving in a dizzying pattern of licks and swirls until Sophie felt herself teetering on the edge. The steady rhythm had just the right pace, just the right pressure. Her back arched again, her entire body quivering as she finally let go.

Feeling Sophie orgasm gave Parker an intense rush of pride. He wanted so much to bring her pleasure. The sound of her cries filled him with a mix of emotions. Lust, desire, joy. Love. His heart raced. *Love? Shit.* He pushed the thought away and brought his attention back to her beautiful body and the fact that she was still trembling.

Slipping her legs off his shoulders, he reached his arms below her waist and gently lifted her into a sitting position. "You okay?" he asked.

Sophie nodded, resting her forehead against his, still breathing hard.

"You're not going to get hiccups again, are you?"

She giggled and shook her head. "I don't think so."

A tremor ran through her, shaking her from head to toe. "Are you cold?"

"I think I am. I was so distracted I hadn't noticed."

The smile on her face sent a rush of warmth through Parker. "Let me get you a towel." He stepped to the side, braced his arms on the edge of the pool and hoisted himself out of the water. He grabbed the blue towel from the top of the pile she'd set out. "Here." He shook it open and draped it around her shoulders, squatting behind her and rubbing her arms with the thick terry cloth.

"Thanks," she said, swiveling and pulling her legs out of the water. "But I have a better idea. Why don't we go take a nice warm shower?"

That was an offer he didn't need to hear twice. He held out a hand to help her up. "Lead the way."

Parker quickly toweled off as he followed Sophie into the house.

"Let's go upstairs," she said, linking her fingers in his. "Bigger shower."

Every inch of Parker's body was on board with this plan as he trotted up the stairs staying behind her just enough to watch as her shapely ass swayed with each step. She flipped on the light in the hall bath, and Parker inhaled a deep breath.

"Wow." He'd been in that bathroom at least a hundred times, but it had somehow doubled in size.

Sophie giggled. "My folks had it redone years ago. One of my dad's legal clients was in construction and couldn't quite pay his bill, so he did a lot of work on the house. This was the best part."

"I'll say." Parker glanced around in awe as he took in the room. The back wall had been knocked out, and in its place was a sunken, two-person jetted tub. Across from that, in the additional space, was the largest shower he'd ever seen. Enormous showerheads graced each wall. A bench lined three sides. Recessed lighting cast a warming glow.

"It's temperature controlled," Sophie said, fiddling with a thermostat on the wall. "How hot do you want it?"

Parker laughed, but it came out more like a huff of breath. His erection strained against the confines of his board shorts. "Hot as you want."

Grinning, Sophie pushed in some numbers and turned on the water. The enclosure turned into an indoor summer rain shower. "Ready?" she asked, stepping toward him and dropping her towel at her feet.

Parker reached behind her and unhooked her bikini top. He'd seen her naked when they'd made love, but the light in her bedroom was far dimmer. With her standing before him, he got a full view of her beautiful breasts. He traced his fingertips around the circumference of one perfect nipple, loving that it immediately stiffened from his touch. Dipping his head, he kissed the puckered flesh, sucking it gently into his mouth as his hands moved south to push down her bikini bottoms.

Sophie sighed, shifting her hips from side to side as the garment fell to the floor. Cool hands slipped beneath his waistband, tugging at the drawstring to loosen it then sliding them past his hips. His erection sprang free, and he pulled her into a hug, needing to feel her against him. Her cool skin pressed against his overheated body sent a shiver straight through him as he strained to get as close to her as possible.

"I think the water's ready," Sophie said, tugging him in the direction of the shower.

The air had begun to cloud as steam wafted around them. Parker stepped under the warm spray, once again marveling at the sheer size of the enclosure.

Sophie tipped her head back, wetting her hair as she slicked it off her forehead. She put a pump's worth of shampoo in her hand and raised her arms to lather. Parker could barely breathe as he watched her breasts rise and fall as she worked the shampoo through. *Does she have the slightest clue how insanely hot she looks?*

When she finished rinsing out the shampoo, she reached for the bar of soap in the cutaway holder, but Parker beat her to it. "May I?" he asked, rolling it between his hands.

The shy smile that spread across Sophie's face made her look like the perfect blend of innocent and drop-dead sexy. He started at her neck, massaging gently. Her eyes closed as she relaxed under his touch, and he had to stop himself from kissing her and pulling her down onto one of the shower benches.

Working as slowly as he could force himself to go, he smoothed his hands lower, soaping her breasts, her waist, slipping his hands between her legs in a gently soapy caress. Sophie moaned at his touch, and the sound was too much. He bent to kiss her, his lips eager to taste her again.

Sophie's mouth sprang open, her tongue twirling around his as she stepped forward, pressing her now warm body to his. Her slick skin seemed to glide against his, rendering his brain all but nonfunctioning.

"My turn," she whispered as she slipped the bar of soap from his hands.

With her mouth still on his, she ran sudsy hands down his chest, around his waist and over his ass, drawing him closer. She stepped toward him, inching him farther under the spray. Her fingers trailed over the ridge of his hipbone, sliding lower until they wrapped around his erection.

Parker gasped as her fingertips grazed his balls on each downward pass. Warm water cascaded over him as Sophie kissed his chest, his stomach. Before he fully realized where she was headed, she dropped to her knees and took him into her mouth.

The sensation knocked what little air was in his lungs straight out of him. Her tongue curled in a slow circle around his swollen tip before tracing a path down his length. Parker reached back to steady himself, his fingers attempting to dig into the tile walls of the shower.

His head fell back in ecstasy as she worked him. Lips, hands, tongue all moving at once. Warm water beat down on him from every direction. The mix of sensations was too much to process all at once, and he gave himself over to every bit of it.

As he neared the point of no return, he forced himself to open his eyes. He glanced down at Sophie. Wet hair cascading down her back, deep red fingernails shining against his skin as she skillfully stroked, full lips closing around him. *Beautiful.* Her eyes opened and she met his stare as her tongue began a devastating assault on the sensitive ridge of skin just beneath his swollen head. The sight of her, eyes locked on his, was too much to bear.

Breathing in deeply through his nose, he attempted to hold off for the last possible second, but he could no longer wait. He reached for her, trying to let her know. "Soph, I'm gonna..."

She linked her fingers with his, and instead of pulling away, she sucked him even deeper into her mouth. His entire body jolted as the orgasm raced through him. Abs tight as fists, balls drawn up so taut they ached, he erupted.

Sophie swallowed hard, continuing to massage him with her tongue, her fingers tight around his, grounding him. Parker's groans echoed around them, reverberating off the shower walls as he shuddered against her.

"Jesus, Soph," he whispered as soon as he was able to speak.

She slipped him out of her mouth, still holding his hands as she rose off the floor. "Good?" she asked, the shy smile back in place.

"There's no word for what that was." He wrapped his arms around her, pulling her into a kiss. Tasting himself on her sweet lips, he melted into her, certain he'd never felt so completely content.

Chapter Sixteen

Parker had been to see more baseball games than he could possibly count. Half of those had been with Joey, but as he drove to the stadium for this one he felt like he was going to see his first game ever. *It's baseball. Just watch the damn game.* He'd have given anything for it to be that simple.

"You okay?" Sophie asked.

He glanced at her as he took the exit toward the ballpark. She looked adorable in jeans and a fitted T-shirt with her hair in two ponytails. Once again she managed to blend her youthful cuteness with her crazy sexiness in a way that left him beyond words. "I'm great."

She tilted her head, studying him, and he could tell she didn't believe him. "We'll have fun." She gave his thigh a squeeze that he felt throughout his body.

"Do you want to go out with Joey after the game?"

"Up to you. We can."

"He mentioned something about it, but I didn't say one way or the other. We'll see how the game goes. If they lose and he's in a foul mood, I'd vote no."

Sophie giggled, the sound easing some of his tension. "Totally reasonable."

Parker pulled into the parking lot, feeling his heart rate accelerate. *Jesus. Settle the fuck down.* For most of his life, arriving at a game was the best experience he could imagine. Today he felt like he was having an anxiety attack.

Hell, he *was* having an anxiety attack. His palms were sweating, he couldn't take a full breath and he had to force himself not to take a U-turn and get right back on the damn highway heading anywhere but the stadium. He parked next to a pillar with the number thirty-three on it, thinking that, given his current state, if he didn't park someplace easily memorable, he'd never find the car again. Duplicate digits were always easier to recall.

"It's hard, isn't it?" Sophie's voice interrupted his thoughts, startling him.

"What?"

"Coming to watch Joey play. It's gotta be really hard. This was your dream too."

Having her see right through him overwhelmed him. "Is it that obvious?"

"Probably not to anyone else."

Parker withdrew the keys from the ignition and turned to look at Sophie. Her eyes were serene, calming him with their sweetness. "Just to you, huh?"

She reached out, her fingers threading through the hair at the base of his neck, massaging with a light touch that instantly lowered his tension level and took his mind at least partially off the game. "I do know you a little better than most people."

"A lot better." Parker closed his eyes, tilting his head back against her hand, letting himself relax. "But if you keep doing that, we're never going to make it out of the parking lot."

A mischievous giggle sounded close to his ear, and he opened his eyes to see Sophie coming in for a kiss. Her lips brushed his softly, but Parker immediately upped the ante, snaking his arm around her waist and drawing her closer as his tongue swept over hers in dizzying circles.

Parker reluctantly pulled back enough to whisper, "The parking lot's looking better by the second, but we should probably go watch the game, shouldn't we?" He half hoped she'd say no. So far this was, without question, the highlight of his day.

"Okay, let's go. But if this game sucks, we're coming straight back to the car. Deal?"

Parker gave her another quick, deep kiss. *God I'm glad she's here with me.* "Deal."

Sophie tried not to fidget as they waited in line at the box office. She knew Parker was tense enough for both of them and she didn't want to add to that. Still, she couldn't help but feel a little nervous. Parker and Joey had not only been each other's best friends, they'd been her best friends. Being with both of them at the same time after all these years was bound to be a little weird.

Good weird. It could be good weird. She tried to convince herself that nothing would go wrong, but a nagging voice argued in her head. *Or it could be the most awkward evening ever. Oh God.*

"You didn't tell him I was coming, right?" she asked.

"Nope." Parker stuck his wallet back in his pocket and held up the tickets. "Kinda want to see the look on his face, don't you?"

The smirk on Parker's face made her smile. "Can't wait."

Sophie followed Parker, her fingers linked tightly in his, as they made their way to their seats. Five rows behind the first base dugout. Sophie had never been inside a major league stadium, but even she realized how great the seats were. "Wow. We could practically reach out and touch the players."

"I think we're about to do just that."

Sophie followed Parker's gaze and saw that Joey had already spotted them. *Well, spotted Parker.*

"You made it," Joey yelled, voice booming as he waved them down to the low wall separating the field from the seats.

Sophie followed Parker, her heart racing.

"Hey." Parker reached out a hand, but Joey closed the distance between them and pulled Parker into an over-the-wall hug.

"You look good, man. Glad to see you."

Sophie stood slightly behind Parker, tugging her jeans down where they'd bunched on her thighs. Her stomach flip-flopped.

Parker turned and gave her a wink. "I brought someone else you might remember." He stepped to the side, reaching his arm around Sophie's waist to pull her forward.

She felt herself flush as she made eye contact with Joey, waiting for the moment of recognition. In typical Joey fashion, his eyes swept up and down the length of her body before he settled on her face. His jaw dropped.

"Well, I'll be fucking damned. Sophie Vaughn." He leaned over the wall and scooped her into a bear hug so hard he lifted her right off the ground.

Holy shit. She laughed, half from nervousness and half from the exuberance of his reaction. "Hey, Joey."

"How the hell are you?" Joey asked, setting her down, but not yet taking his hands off her.

"Good." She glanced at Parker, who eyed them with a look she couldn't quite read. "Really good."

"Still hanging out with goofball?" Joey nodded toward Parker.

Before she could answer, Parker's arm slipped back around her waist. "Yeah, we've been spending a lot of time together."

Surprised by the possessiveness of Parker's hand, she found herself leaning toward him. It felt good. She noticed Joey's glance traveling to her waist then to Parker's eyes. He'd clearly picked up on the meaning and seemed to be processing the information.

"I can't believe you're both here. I gotta get back, but hang out after the game's over, and I'll meet up with you. We'll go out, catch up. Okay?"

Parker gave Sophie a quick look and she nodded. "Sounds good," he said. "We'll be here. Call my cell and tell me where to meet you."

"Will do." Joey clapped Parker on the shoulder and strode away, looking back and catching Sophie's eye for a second before he turned again and joined the other players.

Sophie rubbed Parker's back, trying to gauge how he was doing. "Should we sit?"

"Sure." He gave her a quick squeeze before withdrawing his arm and settling into his seat. "Well, I think we definitely surprised him."

"I'd say so. I thought his jaw was going to hit the floor."

"He looks good. Happy."

Yes. Joey most certainly looked good. Great even. He'd always been a good-looking guy but he'd grown almost unfairly handsome. His classic, Italian features—strong nose and jaw line, intensely dark eyes, caramel-colored skin—all seemed magnified by his long, nearly black hair. He'd managed to have a swagger to his step by the time they'd hit the fifth grade but he seemed to have perfected that over the years as well. There wasn't a woman around who'd taken her eyes off him while he was talking to them.

"What about you? You happy?" She searched Parker's face.

"I'm happy I'm here with you." He smiled and leaned in for a kiss.

A waitress interrupted. "Have you folks had a chance to take a look at the menu? If not I'll come back in a bit."

"You know what you want or do you need a minute?" Parker asked.

"Is it too cliché to say I want hot dogs and beer?"

"Not to me. You still a ketchup girl?"

Sophie's heart fluttered at the fact that he remembered. "Yep."

"We'll take two hotdogs—one ketchup, one mustard—and two beers."

"I'll get those right over to you. Your seats also allow you access to the clubroom, so if you'd like to visit at any point during the game just show your tickets. There's a full bar and buffet, and it's open for the duration of the game."

"Thanks." Parker smiled at the waitress, but Sophie caught the hint of tension in him again.

"I have a confession to make. I can't remember the last time I watched a baseball game."

"You used to come to all the games in high school."

"That's because some of my buddies were on the team." She'd meant it as a compliment, but the darkness clouded Parker's eyes again, and she regretted saying it.

He pecked her on the side of the head. "One of your old buddies is still on the team, and from the looks of the lineup, I think he's the leadoff man."

Sophie's brow furrowed as she squinted at the electronic scoreboard Parker was pointing at. No sooner did she find his name than she heard the announcer say, "Leading off the game will be center fielder Joey Nardo.... Nardo's hitting .315 with a couple of homers and twenty-six stolen bases so far this season."

"Leadoff?" Sophie asked.

"First one to hit." *Jesus. As a rookie.* Parker shook his head to clear it. *Why am I surprised? Solid hitter, super-fast runner.* He'd caught the first few games of the season on TV, before his dad had gotten really sick. Every time he'd watched, Joey had been on fire.

Pride and jealousy battled inside him. Parker shifted in his seat, willing himself to get a grip. "First guy up needs a good hit followed by speed. Joey runs like lightning."

"Is twenty-six stolen bases a lot?"

"Uh, yeah. Not record breaking, but it's damn good."

They stood for the National Anthem, and Parker welcomed the opportunity to focus on something other than the thoughts in his head as he listened to the song.

Their food arrived just as they sat back down. Parker took a long drink of beer and settled in to watch the game.

The teams were evenly matched, keeping the score tied inning after inning. Parker and Sophie cheered extra loudly for Joey but that was hardly necessary. He seemed to have an inordinate number of fans shouting his name. As much as he still loved the game, being there, watching live, was taking more of an emotional toll than Parker had anticipated.

By the end of the fifth inning, Parker was ready for both a break from watching the game and an opportunity to stretch his legs. "You want to go check out the lounge?"

"Sure."

As they made their way through the crowds, Sophie's fingers slipped between his. Her touch warmed him more than he thought possible.

The VIP lounge was bustling. Parker had only been inside the VIP areas at a few stadiums. Once with his dad and Joey as a graduation present, and a few times in college when he and Joey had been able to finagle tickets from various friends.

"Hungry?" he asked.

"A little. Plus I love checking out a buffet. Gives me ideas for weddings."

They perused the spread. There was a seafood table with heaping mounds of shrimp cocktail and enormous crab legs. Two carving stations boasted roast beef and ham. Chafing trays filled with Buffalo wings, assorted pastas and some sort of stuffed chicken breasts graced the remaining tables. He saw Sophie eyeing the dessert table.

"Dessert first?" he asked.

Sophie grinned from ear to ear. "How did you know I was going to suggest that?"

"I'm pretty smart for an ex-jock."

She squeezed his hand. "You're pretty cute too. Now let's get some sugar."

Parker surveyed the table, trying to decide what to take. Sophie went straight for the tower of miniature chocolate-dipped cannoli. "What?" she asked, catching him watching as she placed the third pastry on her plate.

"I didn't say a word."

"I like cannoli."

"So I see."

"You don't?"

Parker tried to remember the last time he'd had one. "I don't know. It's been a long time."

"Let's see if these are any good." She lifted one and took a bite, her tongue sweeping out to catch a bit of filling that caught on the corner of her mouth. "Oh my God. Very good. You have to try these."

She held the other half in front of Parker. Watching her lick her lips, he wanted to drag her and the plate of cannoli into the nearest vacant room. Instead he opened his mouth. Her thumb grazed his lower lip as she popped the pastry into his mouth. Crunchy, creamy, sweet, chocolaty.

"You're right," he mumbled as he chewed. "That's awesome. Grab some more of those."

A plate of chicken wings, two dozen shrimp and several miniature pastries later, Parker felt both full and much calmer. Talking to Sophie was like a magic tonic. He'd never met anyone who was easier to be with. Or more fun.

"I can't believe how many of those you ate," he teased, watching her lick the chocolate from her thumb.

She grinned at him. "Why do you think I make it a point to go to Zumba at least twice a week?"

"So you can eat as many desserts as you want?"

"Can you think of a better reason?"

Parker popped another brownie bite into his mouth. "Not right this second."

Sophie's leg brushed against his under the table, and he felt her ankle lock around his leg. She rubbed her foot against his calf. He'd seen people do that in movies and TV commercials and always thought it looked like such a fake gesture. Like the woman was trying too hard to be some stereotype of sexy. When Sophie did it to him it felt sweet. Intimate. And sexy as hell.

He cupped the back of her head and drew her in for a kiss. Her soft lips molded to his, parting the second his tongue touched them. Feeling her respond, so immediately, so openly, he couldn't think about anything beyond the sensation of kissing her. He breathed her in, her scent, her breath. Her hands slithered around his neck.

For that moment there was no stadium, no room full of people—it was just the two of them.

The eruption of clapping and cheering startled them, and they jumped apart just as the announcement came from every speaker in the room. "A home run for Joey Nardo."

Parker looked up at the nearest TV screen, and sure enough, the instant replay was up showing Joey. "Jesus."

"Cool," Sophie said, still stroking the back of his neck as she leaned closer. Her breath tickled his ear as she whispered. "But Joey's not the only one who's going to score tonight."

The game had been over for half an hour, and Joey had yet to text Parker. Sophie could tell he was getting antsy as he repeatedly checked his phone.

"We can go, you know," she said. "I'm sure we can catch up with him some other time."

"No, it's okay. We said we'd wait. They won, so I'm sure there's tons of press waiting to talk to them." Parker glanced at his phone again just as it lit up with an incoming message. He read aloud. "Taking longer than I thought. Want to head to Godfried's and I'll meet you there?"

"That's fine with me. Why Godfried's of all places?"

Parker shrugged. "My guess is that anywhere near the stadium will not only be packed, but he'll be mobbed by people. Godfried's is mostly locals, less glitzy."

"Tell him we'll see him there."

Parker typed back a message, and they headed for the car. He opened the car door for her, waiting until she was seated before closing it for her too. Had anyone besides him ever done that? Not that she could recall.

She felt so completely safe with him it scared her. Trust wasn't easy for her, even more so since the divorce, yet with Parker she felt safer than she'd ever felt in her life. *Stop being ridiculous.* She knew the beginning of all relationships were smooth sailing. It was way too early to feel so secure and way too early to think that things would stay so blissfully good.

As they drove to Godfried's, Parker slipped his hand into hers. The touch of his fingers sent tingles all through her as his skin skimmed along hers. So light yet so potent. She could have continued having him stroke her palm like that all night.

"Was tonight as bad as you thought it was going to be?" She heard herself ask the question before she thought about it. *What the hell is wrong with me? Am I trying to wreck his mood?*

Parker paused before answering, and Sophie spent the time cursing herself for opening her big mouth.

"No," he finally said. "It really wasn't. It was weird. I don't even know how to explain it. I mean, I'm happy for Joey. Really happy. He's doing exactly what we'd planned to do since we were kids. And he's fucking great at it, just like I always knew he would be."

"But you would have been too."

A wistful smile crossed his gorgeous lips as he shook his head. "Not in the cards."

Her fingers tightened around his. "You're amazing, you know."

Parker snorted. "Because I made it through a ballgame without a nervous breakdown?"

"No. Because most people would have fallen apart if they had to deal with even one of the things you've been through in the past few years, and you...you're... I've never met anyone as strong as you."

"I don't think I'm as strong as you think I am."

"Well, I don't think you realize that I'm always right."

Parker laughed, loud and hard.

He let go of her hand so he could parallel park up the street from Godfried's. "Always right, eh?"

He turned to look at her. His eyes, dark and shining, melted her with their intensity. "Pretty much."

"Then, I guess I'd better listen to you. What was that you said earlier about Joey not being the only one to score tonight?"

Sophie smiled so broadly her cheeks ached. "That was my prediction."

"We'll have to see if that comes true." He leaned closer so slowly it was almost unbearable waiting until his lips reached hers. One soft kiss followed another and then another as he teased her, his nose brushing lightly against hers, his thumbs stroking her cheeks as his fingers sank into her hair.

"You're so definitely going to score tonight." She felt him smile against her mouth as his hands drew her closer. Everything other than Parker simply disappeared.

Chapter Seventeen

Godfried's had remained unchanged since the days the three of them had snuck in together in high school to catch local bands play. One side of the enormous open room held two pool tables, a row of dart boards and assorted pinball machines that were probably way older than most of their clientele. The opposite end had a small platform stage with a tiny dance floor. The wooden floors were worn to the point that they were beveled in spots. It was like a sobriety test. If you could walk across the room without tripping in one of the natural potholes, you were probably still sober.

Parker and Sophie grabbed a table on the game side of the room. It was still loud, but any closer to the band there'd be no chance of being able to hear well enough to carry on a conversation. Parker ordered a pitcher of beer while Sophie headed straight for the old-fashioned popcorn popper and came back with two baskets heaped full of fluffy white kernels.

"Just as salty as I remember," he said, chewing a mouthful.

"Perfect with the beer."

"I got quarters from the waitress. You up for some pinball?"

"Always."

They were still at it at side-by-side machines when Joey arrived.

"Well, if this isn't a freakishly familiar sight," Joey said, striding toward them.

Sophie only let herself glance at him, not taking her eye off the pinball that was snaking its way down the path on the side of the machine. At just the right second she thrust her hip forward and pressed the buttons, sending the ball straight into the super-score hole. Her machine lit up, bells ringing as her score scrolled up by twenty thousand points.

"Ha," she yelped, shooting a glance at Parker just in time to see him get his own super score.

"Ha yourself," he said, laughing as he winked at her.

In the second she let herself get distracted by his wink, she heard the sound of her own ball rolling straight down the center of her machine. She tapped the buttons as fast as she could, but it was useless. "Shit."

"I feel like I'm in a goddamn time machine watching the two of you," Joey said. "Do we have a table, or am I gonna have to stand here and try to beat Soph's score?"

"Table," Parker said, giving his machine a solid knock as his fingers worked lightning fast, getting another high-score spot.

They headed to the table, and Parker slid into the booth. Sophie grabbed her beer from the other side of the table and slipped in alongside him. She handed the empty glass to Joey and poured beer from the pitcher.

"Awesome game, man," Parker said, raising his glass.

Joey clinked his beer against Parker's, and they both drank. Sophie took a sip of hers, feeling like she was witnessing a peace offering between the two of them.

"Thanks. I'm glad you were both there."

"Thanks for getting us the tickets," Sophie said.

"Anytime. Seriously, either of you wants to see a game, just say the word. Sorry it took me so long to get here, by the way. It's crazy how many people want to stop and talk after the game. I don't mind, but at a certain point it's like, dude, look, I wanna get out of here."

Sophie rubbed her hand along the edge of Parker's leg and was happy to feel him press back against her, shifting so his body was angled towards her. He looked much more relaxed than he had at the stadium, and she was relieved. She hated seeing him stressed.

Watching and listening as he and Joey caught up, she couldn't believe she was sitting with the two of them. They were so different than they used to be, yet somehow still the same. One of the pool tables opened up, and Sophie stood.

"Who's up for pool?"

Joey and Parker looked at each other and laughed. "Against you?" Joey said.

Parker snorted. "Not a chance."

"Aww, come on. Neither one of you?"

The guy at the table next to theirs stood up, "I'll play."

Sophie looked the guy up and down. Typical meathead. Big muscles, tight T-shirt, short-cropped hair. He probably thought he was doing her a favor by offering to play. She winked at Parker and Joey. "What do you think, guys?"

"Sure," Parker said, unable to keep from smirking.

"What do you say we make a friendly wager?" Joey said. "He wins, we buy his table another round of drinks. You win, they do the same."

Meathead nodded. "Sounds good to me. Up for it, little lady?"

"It's been a while since I last played, but I'll give it a shot." She strode over to the rack and selected a cue while he racked the balls.

Parker chuckled as he watched Sophie play the meathead. She was hands down the best pool player he'd ever known. The poor guy didn't stand a chance. He tossed a few more pieces of popcorn in his mouth.

"So you and Sophie?" Joey asked.

Parker turned to look at him, eyebrows arched, head cocked. A smile tugged at Parker's lips. "Yeah."

"You fucking dog. What've you been back in town for, a week?"

"A few weeks. And it's not like we didn't already know each other."

"Shit, tell me about it. But I mean, come on. It's Sophie."

The grin returned. "I know. She's awesome."

Joey looked at him with something that could only be described as awe. He shook his head. "Good for you, man. I'll be honest—I was shocked as hell when I saw her standing next to you, but watching you two together, I don't know, it makes sense. You look happy. Both of you."

"We are." Parker took a long swallow of beer and glanced at the pool table just in time to see Sophie sink three balls. The look on the dude's face was priceless. Particularly after she lined up and sank her last shot.

"Looks like we owe your table a pitcher, little lady," he said.

Sophie grinned. "Thanks for the game."

"Not so fast there, what do you say you give me a chance to earn back my self-esteem." He walked over to Sophie and ran his hand down her arm.

Parker instantly bristled.

Sophie took a step back. "Thanks, but I think I'm gonna sit this one out."

"Come on," he said, taking another step toward her.

Parker stood up, allowing Sophie enough space to slide into the booth. "She said thanks for the game. We're just gonna go back to our drinks now."

"I'm just trying to even the score and play with the lady a bit more."

Oh, man, you're asking for it. Parker's legs tensed as he planted them more firmly, prepared to deck the guy. He heard Joey behind him.

"Look, dude," Joey said, his voice calm, "we're just gonna finish enjoying our evening. The lady's with us. Why don't you go back to your friends? Maybe one of them will play with you."

"What'd you say to me?" The guy, straightened to his full height, was easily as tall as Joey but not as muscular. One of his friends got up and came over.

"We have a problem here?" the friend asked, eyes darting back and forth between them. His expression changed from menacing to shocked as he took a closer look at Joey.

"Hey, aren't you Joey Nardo? You are. Man, great game tonight."

"Thanks," Joey said.

"Hey, look who it is. It's Joey Nardo," the guy called to the rest of their friends.

Within seconds there were no fewer than ten people surrounding them, a few asking for autographs.

You've gotta be fucking kidding me. Parker shook his head. *Whatever.* He sat back down next to Sophie.

"Sorry," she said. "You can't take me anywhere."

Parker chuckled. "You're nothing but trouble."

She winked at him. "Thanks for jumping to my defense."

"Don't thank me. Captain Wonderful over there's the one who distracted them all."

"Well, I think you're pretty wonderful." She leaned closer, the sweet smell of her hair wafting around him as he breathed her in.

One kiss told him it was time for them to head home.

Chapter Eighteen

Sophie followed Parker to the front door of his house, remembering how nervous she'd been just weeks before when she'd shown up, chocolate cake in hand. Now a whole different kind of nervous energy coursed through her. Sexual tension had been so thick between them on the ride home she was sure she could actually see it spiraling in the air. Watching Parker fumble with the keys, she wanted to knock him off the porch and into the bushes so she could have her way with him then and there.

The door swung open, and Parker quickly pulled her into the house, slamming the door shut behind them. Before Sophie could even think, his mouth was on hers. Claiming. Possessive. Hungry. His lips were hot and salty, his tongue velvety as he deepened the kiss, pushing her against the foyer wall.

She clasped at his shoulders, tilting her head as he kissed his way to her ear then down to the base of her neck. His fingers passed over her waist and around her hips before heading for the button of her jeans. As soon as he'd flicked it open and slid the zipper down, Sophie wriggled to help him remove them. He went down on his knees, kissing her belly, her hipbone, her thigh, as he tossed her shoes over his shoulder and tugged the jeans off each leg.

His fingers slipped between her legs as he stood, his mouth returning to hers. "Jesus, Soph," he whispered. "You're so wet."

"I told you you were gonna score tonight." She reached between them, giving his erection a firm stroke before she undid his belt and zipper.

Parker moaned as she shoved his jeans down and moved her hand back over him. He was impossibly hard, his skin warm and smooth as silk. He pressed her into the wall again, bending his knees as he lifted her. Sophie clutched at his shirt. She felt him poised at her entrance. Kissing him harder, sucking his tongue into her mouth, she wound both arms around his neck. Parker braced his legs as he pushed up and into her.

The gasp Sophie emitted seemed to reverberate around the two-story entryway of the house. The heat radiating from Parker's body was overwhelming. His need contagious. She locked her legs behind him, feeling the muscles in his ass contracting rhythmically as he thrust inside her.

Sophie kept her shoulders pushed back against the wall. With Parker's chest against hers and his hands on her hips, she could barely move other than to tilt her pelvis toward his on every stroke. That tiny bit of movement was well worth the effort. With each thrust, his pelvic bone ground against her in a way that sent shock waves of pleasure straight through her.

Shaking with intensity, Sophie focused on every sensation. The ease with which he held her up made her feel safe and wanton at the same time. Sex had never felt so passionate or so unbelievably good. She gripped Parker's arms, feeling his muscles flex beneath her fingers. He nibbled her neck, her earlobe, her lower lip, before kissing her full-on, spiraling his tongue against hers. Concentrating on the friction between them, letting her body fill as the pressure built inside her, she thought she might spontaneously combust. Sweat beaded all over her, running down her chest, pooling in her bra.

Parker increased the speed of his movements, and Sophie felt herself cresting on the brink of orgasm. Tightening her internal muscles, she clamped down on him as hard as she could, loving the groan that rumbled out of him. The sound of him coming combined with the increased pressure as he ground his body against her sent her over the edge. He continued thrusting, helping her along.

She cried out, shuddering as she contracted all around him.

Sliding his mouth to her ear once more he whispered, "You're killing me, Soph."

"I hope not," she said, panting against his neck, "because I'd really miss you."

Sophie walked back to her house, the morning sun warm on her face, feeling so happy she wanted to skip. She and Parker had stayed up talking and making love until the sun came up. With only a few hours of sleep, she knew she should be exhausted but instead she felt energized.

The phone was ringing as she keyed into the house and she ran to grab it, tossing her keys onto the kitchen table.

"Hello?" she said, breathlessly.

"You mind telling me where you were all night?" Her father's voice instantly cooled her mood.

"I was at a friend's house." *True.* She picked up a pencil and started doodling on the notepad on the counter. *Why does talking to him turn me back into a twelve-year-old?*

"What friend?"

Sophie's stomach knotted. Her parents had always liked Parker. *Maybe the fact that I was with Parker will make him happy.* She took a quick breath. "Parker Wood."

The pause on the other side of the line gave her hope. "When did you start spending time with him again?"

"A few weeks ago. He moved back into his parents' house after his dad passed away."

"And now you're spending the night with him? I suppose the whole neighborhood sees you sneaking back to our house after your rendezvous?"

Frustrated tears stung the backs of Sophie's eyes. "It's not like that."

"Did you or did you not just get home at ten o'clock in the morning?"

"Yes, I did."

"Was Mr. Thomas out on his porch like he is every morning?"

"I don't know." Her voice was barely audible. She had a hard enough time standing up to her father under normal circumstance. Once he was in lawyer mode she didn't stand a chance.

"When are you going to start thinking about how your behavior looks to other people? Is it not enough that your mother and I had to listen to the entire town talking about your divorce? Now we can expect phone calls telling us you're sleeping around all over the damned neighborhood."

That was too far. "I'm not sleeping around."

"I suppose you were at his house all night playing Parcheesi?"

Anger mixed with her sadness. "No. No I wasn't. But you don't need to make it sound so sordid, Dad. It's not. It's—"

"It's what? Classy? Dignified? For God's sake, Sophie. I'd think you'd have had enough of being talked about after what you've already done."

"What *I've* already done? I'm the one who got cheated on, not the other way around."

"You think people are going to remember that if they see you hopping into bed with every guy in sight?"

"Every guy?" Stomach acid surged up Sophie's throat, making her cough. "Look, I'm not having this conversation with you. You and Mom made it perfectly clear when you moved that you wanted nothing to do with the drama in my life so why don't you just leave this alone. Why are you calling anyway?"

"You're still our daughter and, whether we like it or not, your actions reflect on us."

Sophie crumpled the piece of paper she'd been doodling on, clenching her fist so tightly it ached. "What did you call for?"

"I need you to call the gas company. It's the last account that's still in our name, and they need you to acknowledge that you're taking over the account before they stop sending me the bills. I trust you can make those payments?"

"Yes, of course I can. I'll call them as soon as we hang up."

"Good."

"Anything else?" Sophie wanted to get off the phone so badly she could barely breathe.

"Just try to use some judgment. Please."

Sophie squeezed her eyes shut, willing her brain not to explode. "I do, Dad. I wish you could believe that."

"Act like it, and I'll believe it," he said and hung up.

Chapter Nineteen

Parker's entire body was still humming from his night with Sophie. He felt more alive than he had in years. He'd spent the morning going over invoices and checking in with the crews working various job sites. Just as he'd answered the last email in his inbox, another came through, flagged urgent. Subject heading: *Memorial Dinner for Ethan Wood.*

The temperature in the room seemed to drop by at least ten degrees, as if a ghost had passed by. *A memorial for Dad?* Parker clicked the message.

Dear Mr. Wood,

As you know your father was an important part of this town for many decades. His community service along with his support of all local businesses and his devotion to serving on the town planning board made him a memorable man and one who will truly be missed by all who knew him. To honor his time and commitment a memorial dinner is being held in his honor. A plaque bearing his name will be unveiled and later placed in the town park as thanks for the countless hours he put into restoring it to its original beauty. We would be delighted if you could attend the dinner and ceremony to accept this award on your father's behalf.

My apologies for the short notice, but we wanted to host this event during the summer months while the park is so richly enjoyed by our community.

Thank you in advance for your quick response. We hope to be seeing you at the dinner on July 12 at 6pm at the Hilton Manor hotel.

Our sincere sympathies for your loss.

Best regards,

John Frederickson, Town Commissioner

Parker stared at his computer screen. Dinner? A plaque? It was great that they wanted to honor his dad's service to the town. *Dad would have appreciated that.* But the last thing Parker wanted was to spend an evening with a bunch of people coming up to him and telling him how sorry they were for his loss. He hated that. The look in their eyes. The hands on his shoulder. The sympathy was harder to take than anything else.

Fuck.

Of all the times he wished he'd had a sibling, this one took the cake. But he didn't. And odds were one wasn't going to materialize out of thin air. Certainly not in the next two weeks. *Two weeks. Shit.*

He knew there was no way he could say no. He'd have to go. Hitting reply made his stomach turn.

Dear Mr. Fredrickson,

Thank you for your kind words about my father. I know he'd have been very pleased to know that you all thought so well of him. It would be an honor to attend the dinner.

Best,

Parker Wood

He hit send before he could change his mind.

Parker tried to put thoughts of the memorial out of his mind. Sophie was due to arrive at his house any minute so they could start cooking for the July Fourth BBQ they'd invited Joey to attend. He'd already bought steaks and chicken and had a big pot of water up to boil for the corn. Sophie had said she'd bring dessert and they were going to make potato salad and coleslaw. She was determined to teach him how to cook. He enjoyed any excuse to spend extra time with her, so he'd said "sure".

He saw her walking across the yard, carrying a cooler that looked big enough for her to fit inside. He trotted out and met her halfway, taking the ice chest from her and stealing a kiss. "Jesus, what do you have in this thing? A dead body?"

"Yes, but you weren't supposed to ask. You were just supposed to help me bury it."

Parker chuckled. "You do know it's just the three of us tonight, right?"

"Yep. I also know how much the two of you can eat."

"Good point."

Sophie held the door as he turned sideways to get the cooler into the house. He set it next to the kitchen counter and watched as she unpacked salad, a seemingly endless array of fruits, ice cream, a pie, bacon, eggs, pickles and potatoes.

"We need all this for one meal?" he asked, loving the scowl that furrowed her brow.

"We need a big pot to boil the potatoes." She brushed past him, her hip knocking into his in a way that made him want to order pizza and forget about cooking anything so they could sneak upstairs for a quickie before Joey arrived.

"Yes, ma'am."

Sophie let out a cross between a sigh and a growl as she stuck the ice cream in the freezer.

Parker held up the biggest pot he could find. "Will this work?"

"Sure. Can you fill it about halfway and put it on the stove?"

Sophie put the rest of the groceries in the fridge and set the bag of red potatoes down next to the sink. "You want to scrub potatoes or cut up fruit?"

"I'll do whatever you want." He slipped his hands around her waist, pulling her in for a kiss.

"Oh, really?" She went up on her toes and rubbed her nose against his before kissing him back. "Good to know. For now, how about you quarter some strawberries while I scrub the potatoes."

Parker set the Tupperware full of strawberries on the counter and got a cutting board out of the cupboard. He popped a berry into his mouth.

"Make sure some of those wind up in the fruit salad, okay?"

He grinned. "No promises."

"Oh, hey, I keep forgetting to ask you. I've been invited to an engagement party. It's local and a lot of my friends will be there. Do you want to come with me?" Sophie was trying to act casual, but Parker could hear the nervousness in her voice.

"Sure. Well, wait, when is it?"

Sophie's face fell, and he immediately regretted phrasing it that way. "You don't have to. I mean I know wedding-related stuff can be a bit much and if it's not your thing or you don't want—"

Parker kissed her to stop her from talking. "I want to know when it is because I've got a dinner to attend on the twelfth so if it's that night, I can't go. Any other night, I'm yours."

"Oh." Her cheeks turned a rosy pink as a smile spread across her face. "It's not until the end of next month."

"Then you've got yourself a date."

Sophie looked so happy Parker couldn't help but grin at her.

"What's the dinner you have to go to?" she asked.

"Nothing. I don't even want to go. It's some town thing honoring my dad."

"What kind of town thing?" Sophie stopped scrubbing potatoes and turned to look at him.

Parker continued cutting strawberries. "They're presenting a plaque that's gonna be put in the park. It's at the Hilton. I don't really know much more than that. They just sent me the invitation today."

"Well, let me know when it is, and I'll go with you."

"You don't have to do that," he said. *Shit, I don't even want to go, and he was my dad.*

"I know I don't have to. I want to. I mean, unless you don't want me to."

"It's not that. I'd love to have you there, but I'll tell you right now, I'm not going to be very good company. I hate shit like this. Seriously, if I could think of any good reason to say no, I would have."

Sophie leaned in and kissed him again. "That's why I'm going with you."

That was the nicest thing anyone had offered to do for him in a long time.

"You sure?"

"Positive. That's one of the benefits of having a girlfriend, you know. We do this kind of thing."

Girlfriend? Sure they'd been nearly inseparable for weeks, but she'd never referred to herself that way before. He liked the way it sounded. "Well, boyfriends usually attend 'wedding-related stuff' with their girlfriends, so I guess the rest of our summer is pretty booked up."

"Looks that way." He saw the smile pass back across her face as she returned to scrubbing potatoes.

Sophie crumbled the crisped bacon and sprinkled it over the potato salad, trying to block Parker from stealing the remaining strips from the plate. She smacked his hand as he went for a second piece.

"You're mean," he said, pouting.

She giggled. "That's not what you said last night."

The doorbell rang, and she glanced at the clock. Exactly four p.m. "Wow, he's sure gotten punctual."

She watched Parker cross the kitchen as he headed for the front door. There weren't many things she enjoyed more than the way his ass looked in his low-slung jeans. She tingled from head to toe.

"Hey, Sophie," Joey said, pulling her into a sideways hug and kissing the top of her head. He grabbed a strip of bacon off the plate before she could stop him.

"The two of you are nothing but trouble. Why don't you go get the grill started?"

Joey and Parker both laughed at her reprimand. It was feeling more like the old days by the second.

"What's in the cooler?" Parker asked, pointing to the blue Igloo in Joey's hand.

"My patented margaritas. You got some ice?"

"We sure do."

Watching as they mixed the drinks, it was hard to believe they'd barely talked for two years. They seemed to have fallen right back into their friendship. *Just like we did.* Well, with one

147

notable difference. She felt her cheeks heat. How many times had she hung out with them, cooking for them, wishing she was Parker's girlfriend? Far too many to count. And now it was true. For a second she let her mind wander into the future. Holidays. Weddings. Their wedding.

Whoa. She stopped herself the second the thought crossed her mind. *Way too soon to even think about that.* Hell, he hadn't even told her he loved her yet.

Yet. Would he? Did he? He'd been through so much, what if he just needed to have some fun for a while? Needed the comfort of an old friend and then wanted to move on? It wouldn't be unreasonable. He'd been with Chrissie for so many years, then in recovery. It would be totally understandable if he wanted to live a little. Date tons of women. Play the field.

Oh God. The only thing that had bothered her about learning that he was a virgin was the nagging thought that if they stayed together she'd be his one and only. Nate hadn't been able to stay faithful to her for two months of marriage. How could she possibly expect Parker to be happy with just her for his whole life?

It was almost unthinkable, and yet she wanted it to be possible more than she'd ever wanted anything.

Joey interrupted her thoughts. "Earth to Sophie. You want salt on your margarita?"

She shook her head. "No, thanks." *I need to stop obsessing.*

Parker came up behind her and murmured in her ear. "Where were you just now?"

"Hmm?" she asked, trying to focus on stirring the potato salad.

"You were a million miles away. Joey almost used the BBQ tongs to stir the margarita, and you didn't even notice. You okay?"

"Sorry," she said. "I'm here. I'm fine. He really almost used the tongs?"

"One margarita, no salt." Joey handed her a glass and raised his. "To old friends making new memories."

Parker raised his glass, and all three of them clinked. "I'll drink to that."

"Cheers." Sophie took a sip, savoring the cool lemon-lime liquid as its tanginess filled her mouth. New memories sounded like a great idea.

Parker removed the last steak from the grill and set the platter on the wooden picnic table.

Sophie had been chatting with Joey nonstop. "I see your dad all the time. He seems to be doing well. How's your mom?"

Joey put a heaping spoonful of potato salad on his plate. "She's good. Her MS is really under control now. New meds. She's super busy as usual."

"How many of your brothers and sisters still live at home?"

"Three. Maria and Dave are both still in school. Dave's getting his MBA, and Maria's doing some sort of nursing internship this summer. The rest are still in the house, causing trouble." Joey smiled but he looked bothered about something.

"They're amazing, you know, your folks. My parents had a hard enough time with just me."

"Agreed," Parker said. "I don't think my dad could have handled more than me either. Your parents are goddamned saints."

Joey nodded, biting into an ear of corn. "They are. You know when I got my contract the first thing I offered to do was buy them a new house, and my dad flat out refused. That's your money. You're earning it. You use it. We're fine.'" Joey nailed his father's voice as he mimicked him.

Parker could almost hear the exact same words coming out of Mr. Nardo's mouth over a decade earlier. There had been a baseball camp Joey and Parker both wanted to attend. Best camp in the Northeast and expensive as all get out. With five kids and one on the way, Mr. Nardo hadn't been able to afford the tuition on a mailman's salary.

Parker's dad had offered to pay for both of them, saying it was worth it to him to have the boys together at the camp, but Mr. Nardo wouldn't hear of it. Had it not been for a last-minute grant from the town athletic department, Joey wouldn't have been able to go. Parker wondered if Joey or his dad had ever figured out that the grant had been started that year, or that it had been sponsored in part by Wood Landscaping.

"Be glad your parents are happy for you and want you to do what you want. My dad still treats me like I'm in middle school." Sophie poked at the fruit salad on her plate.

"I thought they moved down to Florida," Joey said.

"They did, but my dad has a way of making his presence known no matter how far away he is."

"Your dad always scared the crap out of me." Joey shoved a forkful of potato salad in his mouth.

"Every man with a daughter hated you. You had good reason to be scared," Parker said, wondering what Sophie's dad was still giving her grief about. He knew they'd had a problem with the divorce, but she hadn't mentioned anything recently. He made a mental note to ask her later.

"True enough." The grin on Joey's face made him look exactly like he had in high school. Handsome, evil and unwilling to take no for an answer to anything.

"I certainly had a few girlfriends whose fathers would have been happy to string you up from the nearest pole." Sophie snorted, shaking her head. "You still leaving a string of broken hearts wherever you go?"

"I don't know about broken hearts, but I haven't settled down yet if that's what you mean."

"No girlfriend?" Sophie asked.

"No one special." Joey eyed Sophie in a way that caught Parker's attention. "Haven't found the right girl. Yet."

She smiled, clearly oblivious to the look Joey was giving her. A look that made Parker's stomach tense. He knew that look. He'd seen it a thousand times over the years. *He still has a thing for Sophie. Not that I can blame him. I do too. But now she's mine.*

The words startled Parker as they formed in his head. *She's mine.* Was she? She'd used the word girlfriend and was inviting him to things like her friend's wedding, but she'd only been divorced for six months. Was she ready to commit to a relationship yet? Was he?

Ready or not, he realized with a swift kick to the head, that he already was. Totally committed. *Holy shit. When did that happen?* Somewhere between a decade-long crush, a first kiss and several earth-shattering nights of passion, his feelings for her had deepened beyond what he'd expected. *Jesus. I'm falling in love with Sophie.*

Joey filled everyone's glasses with the last of the margaritas.

"So good," Sophie said, taking another sip. "Did I hear you say you're looking at houses?"

Joey nodded. "Realtor and I narrowed it down to two. Wanna see?"

"Sure." Sophie scooted closer to Joey as he scrolled through images on his phone. "Oh wow. That's some house."

Parker's stomach tensed as Joey turned the phone so he could see. "Some house" was an understatement. "Nice."

Joey shrugged. "It's a cool place, but I think this one's my first choice."

"Whoa," Sophie said, her eyes bugging. "Is that whole front wall glass?"

"Yep." Joey held the phone out.

The tightness in Parker's stomach seemed to be spreading up through his throat. *I'll never be able to afford a place like that.* He hated himself for thinking that, but it was true. No matter how successful the landscaping business was and how comfortable his lifestyle might be, it would never compare with what Joey had in front of him.

Joey tucked the phone into his pocket and went back to eating. "All I know is whatever house I wind up taking, I'm gonna need a hell of a lot of furniture for it. The stuff in my apartment would barely fill one room of these places."

"I can help with that," Sophie said, a big grin spreading across her face. "I help all my bridal clients set up their wedding registries. I know all the best places for furniture and some awesome interior designers."

Her willingness to help was sweet, yet it set Parker totally on edge. The thought of her spending time helping Joey fix up his bachelor palace was enough to make his already tense stomach turn into a mass of knots. *I can't offer her the same things he can.*

Joey knocked him on the shoulder with the back of his hand. "What about you? You gonna help decorate the new place? Maybe we can go to Spencer's in the mall and get some good posters."

Parker laughed. "You mean you don't still have your old ones?"

"Actually I think I do, in my parents' attic."

"Well, there you go then. Problem solved."

Sophie swatted each of them on the back of the head as she got up to start clearing the dinner plates. "You two are impossible. I'm so taking you shopping before you destroy a perfectly good house with black lights and velvet."

Joey rolled his eyes at Parker. "Women."

Parker tried for a smile. "You gotta love 'em." *Especially this one.*

By the time they'd finished clearing the table and polished off most of Sophie's triple berry pie and all the ice cream, the fireworks started.

Sophie grabbed a blanket and shook it in the air so it tented and lay flat on the grass. "Come on, guys, tradition."

They took their spots on the ground with Sophie between them, watching as the multicolored sprays of light flashed in the sky above the treetops.

"Still the best view of the fireworks," Joey said.

"Best view ever." Parker turned his head to look at Sophie and slipped his hand into hers.

The feel of her skin against his, her fingers slipping between his, made him shudder in spite of the warm humid night.

When the finale came, the entire sky lit up, the ground beneath them shaking from the consecutive explosions. "That was awesome," Joey said. "This is the most relaxed I've been since the season started."

"Good." Sophie gave Parker's hand a quick squeeze before she let go and sat up. "You guys up for a swim?"

"Always," Joey said, tugging off his shirt as he popped up off the blanket. "Last one in's a rotten egg." He took off running toward Sophie's yard.

Instinct almost made Parker run after him, but he didn't.

"I can't believe you're not trying to beat him." Sophie stared at him, her eyes wide with shock.

"Gotta let him win once in a while. Besides, I've already got what I want right here." He pulled her into a kiss that made the fireworks they'd just watched seem like a sparkler on a birthday cake. With her in his arms, he had everything he wanted, which thrilled and terrified him in equal amounts.

Jesus. I'm doomed. And I don't even care. He kissed her harder, pulling her so close the rest of the world disappeared.

Chapter Twenty

Parker had tied his tie three times and the knot still wasn't right. "Fuck." He yanked it off and started again. Over under around and... "Dammit."

"Everything okay in there?" The sound of Sophie's voice startled him. He hadn't realized she'd arrived.

"I can't get this stupid tie right." He stared into the mirror and took a deep breath, raising his arms to try again.

Sophie inserted herself between him and the dresser, her lovely face tilted up at him, eyes clear and calm. "Why don't you let me give it a try? I had to wear a tie every day when I worked at the catering hall. I used to do this for half the employees."

Parker sighed and let his hands drop. "Go for it."

She worked intently, her long fingers maneuvering the slippery fabric. Her hair was pulled back on both sides instead of loose like she usually wore it. It accented her beautiful, heart-shaped face, making her eyes look even bigger, her chin pointier and her cheeks all the more kissable.

"How's that?" she asked, giving the knot a final adjustment as she smoothed his shirt collar down.

Parker stepped to the side and looked in the mirror. In less than two minutes she'd managed to do what he'd been attempting for half an hour. "It's perfect."

Sophie beamed. "You look pretty damned good in a suit."

"You look amazing." His eyes raked over her. She wore a simple black sleeveless dress that wasn't even low cut, but it fit her curves so perfectly she looked sexy as hell. The dress stopped just above her knees, showing off her perfectly shaped calves. Her heels, also plain and black, were so high they made her whole body look different. Her posture was straighter, her center of gravity different, her movements more poised and graceful.

She gave a little curtsy then smoothed her hand over his lapel. Even the slightest touch from her was enough to improve his mood. "Ready to go?" she asked.

His frame of mind instantly darkened. "You know you really don't have to come. This is gonna suck."

Sophie stepped toward him. Standing right in front of him with her sexy pumps, she was still easily six inches shorter than him, but what she lacked in height she made up for in determination. Planting a hand on either side of his face, she tipped his head forward until he had no choice but to look her straight in her crystal-clear eyes.

"I'm going. You're going. We're going." She pulled him forward, giving him a quick, gentle kiss.

Parker would have much preferred throwing off all their fancy clothes and spending the evening in bed but he knew she was right. They had to go. Well, he had to go. And he also had to admit he was glad she was insisting on joining him. For the life of him he couldn't figure out why anyone would volunteer to attend this, but the only thing worse than going would have been going alone.

He plucked his car keys off the dresser and shoved his wallet into his pants pocket. "Let's go get this over with."

Sophie had thought Parker looked tense when they'd gone to the ballgame. Compared to how he looked tonight, that was nothing. They drove to the Hilton in total silence. The few times she'd attempted to start a conversation, he'd made it clear he couldn't handle small talk, and if she said anything encouraging, all it seemed to do was make him cranky.

Stay quiet. Give him space. Keeping quiet wasn't Sophie's strong suit. Nervous energy made her chatty, and she was nervous for Parker. She'd never lost a parent, so she didn't entirely know what he was going through, but she had some idea.

He'd never known his mom. She'd had complications during his delivery and had died a few days after he was born. All his life, it had been Parker and his dad. Sophie had never known anyone with a closer relationship with either of their parents. Not only was Mr. Wood proud of everything Parker did, the two of them seemed to actually be buddies. Losing him had to be tearing Parker apart, but he couldn't seem to talk about it.

Sure, he'd mentioned missing him. He'd said he couldn't deal with cleaning out his room yet or getting rid of his stuff. But she hadn't seen the emotions tugging at him. Not until today.

"It's not too late to change your mind," he said as he pulled into the parking deck.

"Will you please stop saying that?"

"Fine."

Fine. That was the third "fine" she'd gotten out of him.

She hated that word. Hated all monosyllabic answers. They reminded her of her father. And her ex. *Give him a break. He's just having a rough night.* She knew that was true. He never clammed up like this. Circumstance was to blame.

He fidgeted with his tie. She wasn't sure if it was too tight or he was attempting to straighten it, but all he'd succeeded in doing was making it crooked. *Tell him.* "You're...it's off to one side now. May I?"

"Fine."

Sophie sighed, trying not to shake her head as she reached up and adjusted the knot. "Perfect."

"Good."

Well, at least that's better than "fine". She followed him across the parking deck to the elevator. His hands were shoved into his pants pockets, making his jacket bunch up. She'd never seen anyone look more uncomfortable in a suit. *I need to get him to have a drink. The sooner the better.*

Inside the elevator he stared at the numbers as they lit up above the door. He looked like he was going to his own execution instead of a fancy dinner. When the door to the elevator slid open, they were greeted by a poster set on an enormous easel. *Ethan Wood Memorial Banquet* the sign read atop a giant photo of Parker's dad.

The tension that had been holding him so taut seemed to drain out of him the second he saw the image. His shoulders slumped. The tight set of his jaw slackened. All she saw was sadness. Her heart ached. She wanted to throw her arms around him and tell him everything was going to be okay. Knowing that would be out of place she kept herself in check. Unsure how he'd react to any physical contact, she let her hand brush against his. Relief swept over her as he slipped his fingers between hers and gave them a tight squeeze.

A white-haired gentleman who looked vaguely familiar strode toward them. "Parker, so glad you could make it."

"Thanks, Mr. Brown." He let go of Sophie's hand and reached out to shake Mr. Brown's.

"Who's this lovely young woman?"

"This is Sophie Vaughn. We grew up together. She knew my dad really well."

"Pleasure to meet you, Ms. Vaughn. Parker, I'd like to introduce you to the presenters before the ceremony begins if that's okay with you."

"Sure." Parker's hand slipped back into his pocket instead of back into Sophie's. "Why don't you go find our table?"

"Okay." Sighing, she made her way into the ballroom. *This is going to be a very long night.*

Parker willed himself to be as numb as possible as he met the lineup of people who would be speaking about his father. *Just get through it and then it'll be over.* That's how he'd viewed every surgery, every new physical therapy challenge, every other painful event he'd had to face. *Just do it.* Not what Nike had been referring to, but sound advice nonetheless.

Roughly half the men were people Parker had met before. He'd spent enough time working at the landscaping business that he'd had contact with the majority of them over either jobs or charity events or both. The few people he didn't know were friendly enough. Everyone full of kind words about his father. Kind words and sympathy. *That look in their eyes.* That was what was going to make Parker lose it.

He'd purposely kept the funeral small and private, wanting to deal with as few people as possible. And there he'd been able to keep his sunglasses on the entire time. Behind the dark lenses it was much easier to keep it together. No one could tell if he was making eye contact or not. No one could see that tears were welling up. He didn't have to worry about the pain being quite so obvious. Without them, he felt like he was wearing a flashing arrow that said "hurting".

"Parker, this is Jarrod Weston. He took over the Park Commission when Bill Thompson stepped down last year."

Jarrod Weston. The name rang a bell but not in conjunction with anything work related. *Don't even...* He looked up to see a thin blond man in an Armani suit approaching, hand extended. *Fuck. Me.* It was the asshole who had married Chrissie.

159

Parker's jaw tensed so tight he thought he might actually crack a tooth. He shook Jarrod's hand in silence, managing nothing more than a quick nod. Jarrod didn't meet his eyes. *Chicken shit.*

"Jarrod will be presenting the actual plaque, so we'll need the two of you for photos afterward. They'll tell you both where to go to have those taken."

Clearly Mr. Brown had no idea about their history. The lightheartedness with which he spoke seemed almost comical in comparison to the turmoil Parker felt. Someone stepped to the podium at the front of the banquet hall and asked that everyone please take their seats.

Parker saw Sophie sitting at the table closest to the podium. She was scanning the room, and he knew she was looking for him. The thought comforted him. He knew he'd been giving her a hard time. He wasn't trying to, but it seemed to keep happening anyway.

Truthfully, he was very thankful she was there. *I need to tell her that. Now.* Parker's thoughts were interrupted with a sight that knocked what little air he had in his lungs right out. At the table next to his, seated with the other presenters and their wives, he saw an unmistakable head of blonde hair. As if she felt his eyes on her she turned, and looked straight at Parker. *Chrissie.*

The urge to walk straight out of the room was nearly overwhelming. Instead, Parker made it to the open seat beside Sophie. She smiled when she saw him, scooting her chair to the side so he could sit, but that wasn't meant to happen yet. Before he could slip into the chair, Chrissie stood and walked over to him.

She looked different. Older. And by far more than the two years since he'd seen her. Her features had lost their girlishness. Her nose seemed pointier, her eyes deeper set, her lips thinner. She was still beautiful, but something was
160

missing. The spark that had been her defining quality seemed to be gone, replaced with a solemn poise.

"Parker," she said, reaching up to touch his shoulder and placing a kiss on his cheek.

He stiffened at her touch, trying not to pull away too rudely, but wanting to remove himself from her reach nonetheless. "Hey," was all he could manage.

"I'm so sorry about your dad. He was such a nice man."

"Thanks." Parker pulled out his chair, trying to give her the clue that it was time to sit down and not make small talk. He caught the look on Sophie's face. Her eyes were wide as they darted between him and Chrissie.

"We should talk later, after the ceremony," Chrissie said.

"We'll see. I don't think we plan on sticking around for very long." He nodded at Sophie, who smiled up at him.

Chrissie followed his gaze and seemed to realize he was there with a date. "Oh, I'm sorry, I didn't mean to be rude. Hi. I'm Chrissie Weston." She held out her hand.

Parker shook his head. *Holy God.*

"I know," Sophie said, taking her hand and staring her straight in the eyes. "Sophie Vaughn."

Chrissie's eyes bugged to cartoonish size as the name registered. "Oh. My. God. Sophie. You're the last person I would have expected to run into here."

"Likewise," Sophie said, shooting Parker a quick glance.

"How are you? You look great."

"So do you. I'm good, thanks, but I think they're trying to get the ceremony started."

Chrissie looked up at the podium just as the speaker tapped the mic. "You're right." She swept a hand across Parker's shoulder and gave it a quick squeeze. "We'll catch up later."

Catch up later? What the fuck is she talking about? Parker was about to whisper something to Sophie but the speaker cleared his throat and began to talk.

"I'd like to thank you all for coming tonight to honor a man who meant so much to our community and so much to everyone in this room. Let's start with a moment of silence in memory of Mr. Ethan Wood."

The room fell completely silent. Parker's heart beat hard enough that he was certain everyone at the table could hear it. He didn't need a moment to remember his dad. He thought about him every day whether he wanted to or not. The urge to get up and leave returned with almost overpowering strength.

Sophie reached over and took his hand. The simple act of kindness brought him so much relief he thought he might start crying. *Get. A. Grip.* He forced himself to breathe. *Jesus. She's just holding my hand. That guy's just saying words. Calm the fuck down before you make an ass of yourself in front of the whole damned town.*

As much as he wanted to hang on to Sophie's hand, he shifted his position and let it go. He reached for his water glass and took as much of a drink as he could manage to swallow. The cool water passed over the lump in his throat and spiraled down into his stomach.

For what seemed like an eternity, he listened as speakers got up, one after another, saying the kindest things about his father he could imagine hearing. Parker bit down on his tongue more than once to focus on the pain of the bite rather than the pain of his memories. By the time they were ready to present the plaque, he wasn't sure he could stand let alone walk to the front of the room. His shoulders were so tense he could barely move.

Seeing Jarrod Weston, of all people, up there holding the plaque, Parker felt as if he might throw up. At least the disgust he felt for Jarrod was something to focus on that had nothing to do with his father. This was the asshole who'd taken Chrissie from him. The catalyst that had inadvertently changed every plan he had for his life. Watching him, smug and dapper, with his well-coiffed hair and expensive suit, Parker felt nothing but disdain.

"And so, in honor of the many great services he provided for our community, I'd like to present this plaque, which will be placed in Hunter Park beside the fountain Mr. Wood helped restore to its original glory." Jarrod pulled a drawstring, and the blue velvet curtain that had covered the plaque fell away, revealing a large flat slab of granite with an engraved plate on it.

"If Mr. Wood's son, Parker, wouldn't mind joining me..."

Parker pushed his chair away from the table and focused on putting one foot in front of the other. Jarrod shook his hand and stepped aside, and Parker realized he was expected to speak. *Christ.* He breathed in through his nose. *Keep it simple. Speak from the heart.* He knew that's what his dad would have told him to do. He exhaled slowly.

"Giving back to the community was always a top priority for my father and I know this would have meant a great deal to him. It certainly means a lot to me. Thank you for honoring him." He held his breath, hoping that was enough.

Applause echoed through the room. Parker looked out at the audience, focusing on nothing until he caught Sophie's eye. She stared directly at him, calm and steady. He'd never been more grateful for anything than for her presence at that moment. Her eyes were like a safe harbor. A port in a storm. He held her gaze until he returned safely to her side.

As he took his seat he leaned in and gave her a quick kiss, not caring who was watching. When he pulled away, he saw that the one person who seemed to have noticed was Chrissie. She raised an eyebrow and quickly turned back to Jarrod.

Karen Stivali

Before Parker could say anything to Sophie, a waiter arrived between them. "Can I get you a drink from the bar?"

"Yes, Sophie?"

"I'll have a glass of white wine."

"Vodka, please, on the rocks with a twist of lime."

The waiter nodded and moved to the next couple at the table.

Sophie leaned closer to Parker, her sweet scent soothing him. "You did great."

"Really? I don't even remember what the hell I said."

"Trust me. It was perfect." She rested her hand on his leg, her touch warm and comforting.

"Thanks."

Parker tried to focus on eating dinner, but during every course someone came over to pay condolences, offer a story about how his dad had been such a great guy or put a reassuring hand on his shoulder. By the time the main course was over, Parker felt like he'd been at the banquet for a year.

"I'm gonna go grab another drink at the bar. Can I get you anything?"

Sophie shook her head. "No, thanks. I'm good. You want me to come with you?"

"No, there's not even a line. I'll be back in a minute."

He headed to the bar, ordered a beer and stuck a dollar in the tip jar. His leg ached, and he tried to stretch and relax the muscles like Tanya had taught him. Just as he felt it starting to loosen up the tiniest bit, he heard Chrissie's voice.

"So, you and Sophie are...a couple?"

Parker gripped the neck of the beer bottle and took a sip. "Yes, we are."

Chrissie gave a shrug that set Parker's teeth on edge. "That's...unexpected."

"Yeah, well, people surprise each other all the time." The harshness in his tone surprised even him. He'd thought his anger toward Chrissie had dissipated with time, but now that she was standing in front of him, he could feel it percolating again.

He looked at her, waiting to see if she'd have a response, hoping she'd go back to her husband and leave him alone. He had enough to deal with tonight without adding her to the mix.

"I'm sorry, Parker. You have no idea how sorry I am. I must have written you three-dozen letters in the past couple of years, trying to tell you how bad I feel about how we ended. About what I did. I just really hope you know that I realize how awful I was. And I... It's...I always..."

Jesus. Is she starting to cry? Not wanting to draw any more attention than necessary, he grabbed a few napkins off the bar, shoved them into her hand and took her by the elbow to lead her to a more out-of-the-way location.

"What are you talking about?"

Chrissie dabbed at her eyes. "I'm talking about me. About how I screwed everything up so royally. I was an idiot, Parker. I had no idea what I was doing or how it would all turn out, for all of us."

"Well, they say everything happens for a reason. Everyone's fine now. Let's just move on, okay?" *Like right now. Move on from this conversation. End this entire nightmare of an evening.*

"Are you fine? Because I'm not."

"What are you talking about?"

"I didn't have to come tonight. I don't usually go to these things with Jarrod. I came because I wanted to see you."

"Why?"

Chrissie looked at him, her eyes surrealistically blue like they always were when she cried. "I miss you."

He was neither expecting nor prepared to hear those words. "Miss me? You threw me away two years ago. You never once called while I was in the hospital."

"I made a mistake." She looked up at him, eyes now red. "I'm sorry. And I have to go. Jarrod's looking for me."

Before Parker could get in another word, she disappeared into the crowd of people, leaving him wondering what had just happened. *What the hell was she trying to say? A mistake?* Parker shook his head. It didn't matter. Chrissie was the past, and he'd worked long and hard to put her and everything else about that time in his life behind him.

He started back to the table, wanting nothing more than to find Sophie and see if they could possibly sneak out and go home. Halfway there, Mr. Brown flagged him down.

"Parker, we're ready for those photos now. Jarrod needs to get home. Something about his babysitter. Can we get those shots now?"

Scanning the crowd for Sophie, he saw her sitting at the table, alone, not looking any more pleased than he felt. He tried to make eye contact with her, but she didn't look up. "Will this be quick?"

"Should only take a few minutes. The plaque's been moved to the lobby. Follow me."

Giving Sophie one last glance, he trailed Mr. Brown, wanting nothing more than to finish up this last obligation and get the hell out of this event.

Shaking hands with Jarrod with what he hoped was some semblance of a smile on his face was even more of a challenge than Parker expected. His entire body ached from both stress and from the strain of faking his way through everything for an entire evening.

"Thanks, gentlemen. You can look for these in the paper and the town newsletter. Parker, you'll be notified when the plaque is actually placed in the park. Just a small ceremony. We hope to see you there."

Take your time. That's what he wanted to say. Instead he said, "Thank you, sir. I appreciate all you've done on behalf of my father."

He made his way back into the banquet room and didn't see Sophie anywhere. She wasn't at their table, wasn't at the bar. *Did she leave? She couldn't. I drove.* He was about to head toward the lobby to see if she was there when he saw her walk in through the far door.

"There you are," he said. "Please tell me you're ready to go."

"More than ready." There was an edge to her voice that hadn't been there earlier.

"You okay?" he asked.

"Fine," she said.

"Okay, let's go."

Sophie sat in silence once again as Parker drove them home. He seemed less tense but was obviously deep in thought. Her heart beat unevenly as she wondered what had him so pensive. Memories of his father...or of Chrissie?

Hating the jealousy she felt, she tried to rationalize. *He didn't know she was going to be there. He'd certainly looked surprised to see her. And less than pleased. But still.* She couldn't shake the image of him taking Chrissie by the arm and leading her off to chat.

They were together for so many years. There must be countless unresolved issues between them. What if he still has feelings for her? What if... It was too horrible to complete the thought.

Nate had cheated on her after only two months of marriage. And he'd had dozens of girlfriends before her. How could Parker possibly be content with her as his one and only? The likely answer scared her to death. *He probably can't.*

"You want to come to my house or should I take you home?"

Oh God. In all the nights they'd spent together, he'd never phrased it like that before. *Does he even want to spend the night with me or is this him giving me the brush off?* She felt their entire meal sitting in her stomach, churning at an alarming rate.

"What do you want?"

"I just want this night to be over," he said.

Well, there's my answer. "Take me home."

Parker pulled into her driveway and put the car in park. He reached for the keys to turn off the ignition. "Don't bother," she said, undoing her seat belt and fumbling with the door handle.

"What do you mean don't bother?" Parker turned the key and put his hand on her arm. "Are you pissed at me?"

Pissed. Hurt. Exasperated. All she could do was grunt as she managed to get the car door open and climb out of his Land Rover. She slammed the door and walked up her front path as quickly as she could in her stupid high heels.

She heard his door slam. "Sophie, what the hell…"

Her hands were shaking so badly she dropped her keys on the front porch. By the time she'd picked them up he was standing beside her.

"What's going on with you?" he asked.

She stared up at him. He looked completely bewildered. "What's going on with me? I'm not the one who's been cranky as shit for the past few days. I'm not the one who couldn't say two consecutive words all night."

Parker ran his hand through his hair and paced a few steps away. "I'm sorry. You know I didn't want to go to this thing. I've had a lot on my mind."

"I know. That's why I didn't say anything. I tried to be supportive. I kept telling myself it wasn't me. You were just upset. Then I noticed that it was just me you seemed to be having a hard time talking to. You had plenty to say to Chrissie." Sophie's chest tightened to the point that she wondered if maybe she was having a heart attack.

"Chrissie? What are you talking about?"

"When you went to get that drink and you didn't come back after a few minutes I went looking for you. I thought maybe you were upset and needed to leave or needed to be rescued from some overzealous guest who was talking your ear off. Instead I found you huddled deep in conversation with Chrissie. It seemed like you had plenty to say to her."

"She was doing all the talking, trust me."

Trust me. He couldn't have asked for her to do anything more difficult than that. "I just...never mind."

"Look, I didn't want to be talking to Chrissie any more than I wanted to be at this whole event. And, if you recall, I told you a hundred times you didn't have to come."

A loud growl rumbled out of her. She fumbled with her key ring, desperate to find the house key.

"You're right. You did. And stupid me, I didn't listen. All I could think about was you and how hard it was going to be on you and how I wanted to be there for you because that's what you do for people you love." The second the words came out of her mouth she nearly dropped the keys again. *Oh, fuck.*

Parker stopped pacing, and she could feel him staring at her. "You love me?"

Sophie felt cold from head to toe with the exception of her burning-hot cheeks. *Oh God. What's wrong with me?* She

169

considered saying no, but every last bit of bravado had drained out of her body.

"Yes, okay? I love you. Are you happy now?" *Asshole.*

To her complete dismay he started laughing.

"You're an idiot," she said.

"No argument. But I'm an idiot who's very much in love. With you."

The keychain clattered to the ground. "What?"

"Sophie, I'm sorry. You're right. I've been a pain in the ass and moody as shit and I have no idea how you put up with me, but I'm glad you did. And I'm sorry I was being a dick tonight, I really am. Jesus, when you got mad, I thought you'd finally realized I was too fucked up and were giving me the brush off."

Sophie bent and picked up the keys, fidgeting with them to avoid looking at him. Her heart drummed so fast she couldn't even count the beats.

"Look at me," he said, tucking a finger under her chin and tilting her face up toward his. "I should have told you this weeks ago, but I didn't want to look like a total dork."

"Should have told me what?" Her voice came out so softly she wasn't even sure she'd said the words out loud.

"That I'm so in love with you I can barely see straight. That spending time with you is the best part of my day, every day, and that the days I've spent with you are the happiest I've had in as long as I can remember. I love you, Sophie."

Chapter Twenty-One

Saying the words out loud made Parker feel bold and vulnerable at the same time. He held his breath as he waited for her to respond. Anything other than pulling away would be good. Having her angry at him had made him realize just how much he didn't want to lose her. *Say something. Anything. Please.*

She held his gaze, features still clouded with uncertainty. "Do you really mean all that?"

"I promised you, Soph, I'll never lie to you. I love you."

A tear rolled down her cheek and over his hand. "I love you too."

Parker swallowed hard letting her words sink in. *She loves me too.* He stroked her cheek with his thumb, brushing away the tear then kissing the trail it left on her face. Sweet. Salty. Warm. She tasted like home. His lips grazed hers in a gentle pass. Once. Twice.

She took a step toward him, rising up onto her toes, her fingers sinking into the hair at the back of his head, her mouth opening beneath his. Parker deepened the kiss, his tongue caressing hers as his hands pulled her closer. Kissing Sophie always felt amazing, but this kiss felt heavenly. He breathed her in, letting her words repeat in his head. *I love you too.*

Reluctantly he pulled away, resting his forehead against hers, eyes still closed, not wanting to break the spell that seemed to surround them. "I'm thinking maybe we should go in the house."

Sophie giggled, her sweet breath soft against his lips. "I think you're right. But I seem to be having trouble with these tonight." She placed her keys in his hand.

Parker grinned as he unlocked the door and held it open. Sophie tossed her purse on the hall table and started toward the kitchen. "Do you want a drink? I'm dying of thirst."

"Water would be great." He hadn't realized how parched his throat had become until she asked.

Watching her get glasses out of the cupboard, his eyes raked over her sexy silhouette. Heat spread throughout his body. She grabbed ice out of the freezer, dropping the cubes into both glasses before filling them.

She took a sip from one as she handed him the other. He gulped down two mouthfuls then set it down, tugging her closer.

Her lips were cool and firm under his as he pressed her against the cabinets. She teetered, and he realized she was still wearing her heels. Wrapping his hands around her tiny waist, he lifted her up onto the kitchen counter. He heard her shoes drop to the floor as her legs wrapped around him.

"Is it hot in here?" she asked.

"No, it's you." Parker fished a chunk of ice out of his glass and held it to her lips.

The sight of her tongue rolling over the crystal cube was enough to make his knees go weak. "Better?" he asked.

She shook her head, her hair sweeping from side to side, filling the air with her honeyed scent. "Not yet."

He trailed the cube down the side of her neck, loving the way she shuddered. "How about now?" He drew it slowly back and forth just below her collarbone.

"Little bit." Her voice quivered as she arched her neck.

He dipped his head down, kissing his way along the trail of cool water, sucking on the tender spot at the base of her neck until she groaned. His erection strained against the confines of his trousers, but he was far from ready to stop teasing her. Reaching behind her, he slid the zipper slowly down her back.

Sophie shrugged, and the dress fell off her shoulders, pooling around her hips on the granite counter. She wore a black bustier he'd never seen before. It had thin, silky straps and red satin trimming the tops of both bra cups. Red laces crisscrossed their way down the center of her body, making her look like a gift he couldn't wait to unwrap.

Parker ran the ice cube along the swell of each breast. She drew in a short breath, her mouth falling open. *So fucking sexy.* He traced the ice up and down the midline of her chest, watching as droplets ran straight down her cleavage.

She shivered again as he pulled one of the red laces, undoing the bow. He worked the ties loose with his finger then gave a sharp tug so the entire string pulled free. Sophie gasped as the corset fell open. He forced himself to swallow, a less than easy task when all he wanted to do was push her down onto the counter and climb on top of her.

He eased the narrow straps off her shoulders until the lingerie joined her dress on the countertop. Dragging the ice across her breast, he watched as her flesh puckered. He drew circles around each tightened peak before trailing his way down to her belly. "Cooler yet?" he asked, his lips closing over one taut nipple.

"No," she rasped.

He dipped the ice into her belly button as he sucked harder.

"Yes," she said.

He no longer cared what question she was answering, he just loved hearing the word escape her lips. *Yes.* Scooping her off the counter, he headed for her room.

The second he placed her on her bed, she wriggled the rest of the way out of her dress. Seeing her there, naked except for the tiniest black panties with a little red bow, Parker couldn't wait any longer. He climbed on top of her, not caring that he was still fully clothed. He tugged at the knot on his tie just enough to loosen it then struggled out of his jacket and tossed it off the edge of the bed. Placing his hands on either side of her, he kissed his way from her belly to her lips sliding his body back and forth on top of hers.

Even through his trousers he could feel the intense heat as he rubbed against her. She groaned into his mouth as he swiveled his hips. Her legs wound around his body, pulling him to her.

"Feels so good," she whispered.

Wanting to make her feel even better, he eased himself up. He hooked his fingers under the edge of her panties, and she raised her hips to help as he slid them over the full curve of her ass. Lifting her legs, he slipped them the rest of the way off and tossed them aside.

Sophie moaned as he ran his hands down her thighs. She reached for him, fingers working to undo his belt buckle. With a firm yank, the belt slid out of his belt loops and joined the other garments on the floor. Parker sighed with relief as Sophie's fingers curled around his erection. He craved her touch but was determined to focus on her pleasure.

He rubbed the heel of his hand against her, feeling her wetness coat his palm. "Jesus, Soph."

She rocked against him, making it next to impossible to combat the desire to plunge inside her. Spiraling his thumb against her, he felt her starting to quiver beneath him. "That's it. Let it go, baby. Come for me."

Sophie tipped her head back, eyes tightly closed, hips arching off the bed as she gave in. *Holy hell.* He slowed his movements, waiting for her to ride it out. He ached to be inside her. Leaning forward, he lowered his mouth to hers. No sooner did his lips touch hers than she hiccupped.

"Oh God," she groaned, her hand covering her mouth as she hiccupped again.

Parker snorted with laughter. "Hang on." He reached over the edge of the bed, trying to contain his reaction to his erection pressing into the soft flesh of her thigh. Sweeping his hand back and forth under the bed, he found what he wanted.

"Ta-da." He held up a jar of peanut butter.

Sophie laughed so hard the bed shook. "Where on earth did you get that?"

Grinning so wide his cheeks hurt Parker unscrewed the lid. "I stashed it a few weeks ago. In case of emergencies such as this. There's one in the nightstand at my house too."

Giggles and hiccups poured out of her. "You're crazy."

"I prefer the term 'prepared'. Shit. I forgot a spoon. Oh well." He swirled his index finger deep inside the jar. "Open wide."

Sophie hiccupped then parted her lips. Parker slipped his finger between them. She rolled her tongue, sweeping the peanut butter off, then gave a suck so hard he felt it straight through every muscle in his torso. He twitched against her belly, his arousal leaving streaks of wetness across her skin.

Groaning, he slowly withdrew his finger. He forced himself to breathe so he could stay in control of the orgasm that was threatening to arrive way before he wanted it.

As she chewed the mouthful, Parker dipped his finger in the jar again. "Good? Or you need some more?"

Her tongue darted out, licking a dab from the corner of her mouth. "Not sure yet."

"Maybe you need some here." He ran his finger down the right side of her stomach, then in two swirls on either side of her belly button and in a curve on her left side.

Her eyes widened as a smile tugged at her lips. "Did you just write *I <3 U* in peanut butter?"

"Maybe." He bent forward and licked the *I* from bottom to top then traced his tongue along the path of the heart and *U*.

"I love you," she said.

"I love you too." He kissed her, slow and gentle, as he eased his body down against hers. His erection nestled against her warmth.

Sophie rocked beneath him, her hand slipping between them to guide him inside her. Sinking into her, his mind swirled. She sucked on his lower lip, nipping at him with her teeth. *So good. How can anything possibly feel this good?*

She tugged at his shirt, pulling the tails out of his trousers and running her hands up his back. Her fingernails scratched over his skin, sending ripples of electricity straight to his groin. He ground against her, sliding his hand beneath her hips, tugging her closer on every thrust. Feeling her start to shake, he braced himself against the mattress, swiveling harder with every upward movement. Her nails dug into his back as she cried out.

Sophie's warm breath against his neck coupled with the pull inside her was more than he could stand. His body jerked forward as the orgasm tore through him, shaking him to his core. Panting, he rolled them both onto their sides. He brushed her hair behind her ear, kissing her eyelids, her nose, her lips.

"No hiccups this time?" he asked.

She giggled, still out of breath. "I don't think so."

"Good, because I'm pretty sure the peanut butter jar rolled off the bed at some point."

"Oh God. Speaking of peanut butter, I think you're going to need to take these clothes to the dry cleaner."

Parker laughed. "I think you're right." He sat up and unbuttoned his shirt, tugging at the sleeves, then he stripped off his pants, dropping them all in a heap alongside the bed. As he lay back down, he pulled Sophie to him, spooning his body around hers. Nestling his nose in her hair he whispered, "Thanks for coming with me tonight."

She drew his hand to her lips kissing his palm. "Thanks for letting me."

Chapter Twenty-Two

Parker couldn't remember a time in his life when things had been going more smoothly than they had for the past month. Ever since the banquet, everything seemed to have fallen into place. Work was great. New contracts poured in, crews completed jobs ahead of schedule and Parker finally felt as if the business was his. He and Joey had been hanging out regularly, and things had started to feel like they used to, easy and natural. As for Sophie, things couldn't have been better. Waking up with her by his side nearly every morning made him feel like the luckiest man in the world.

He dug his shovel deep into the ground in an attempt to loosen a particularly stubborn rock. The miniature Japanese Maple in Sophie's front yard needed to be moved before it died, and Parker had promised her he'd take care of it. He missed working outdoors now that most of his time was spent managing the office end of the business. The warm, late-summer breeze spiraled around him, sweet with the scent of the wisteria that bloomed along the side of the house.

Just as the rock gave way, Parker heard a car pull into Sophie's driveway. Looking up, he saw a tall man get out of the car and slam the door. He strode past Parker without saying a word and trotted up the front steps of the house.

Parker stood, wiping his hand on his jeans as the man pounded on the front door. "Can I help you?" he asked.

The guy barely turned his head in Parker's direction. "No."

Who the hell is this asshole? Parker felt the hairs on the back of his neck stand up as he realized. *Shit. It's Sophie's ex.*

He'd seen a picture or two, and now that he was standing close enough to get a good look, it was clearly him. Short-cropped brown hair, thin lips, arrogant from head to toe.

The front door swung open, and Parker caught the look on Sophie's face as she laid eyes on Nate.

"I can't believe you're doing this," she said.

"I'm doing this? You're the one who won't let this go."

"I'm not discussing this with you. My lawyer sent your lawyer the papers. Sign them, or I'll take you back to court."

Nate raked both hands through his hair. "I'm not signing. You'll sell that timeshare over my dead body."

Sophie shrugged. "If you insist."

"Dammit, Sophie. We've talked about this a million times. If we sell right now, we lose money. I'm not doing it."

"I don't care if we lose money. I don't care what happens to the timeshare. I just want my half, now. If I don't put a down payment on that new storefront, I'm going to lose it. I need the cash, not a timeshare with you. You don't like the idea of selling to the buyer I found? Fine. Buy out my half."

"No."

Sophie closed her eyes. "That's why you're dealing with my lawyer."

"You're such a goddamned bitch."

Parker's stomach tensed. "Hey. Apologize to the lady."

"Excuse me?" Nate walked down the porch steps as Parker moved toward him. "Who the hell do you think are? Mind your own fucking business."

Parker's nostrils flared. "Sophie is my business."

Nate gave him a smug look up and down. "Is that so? She hired you as a bodyguard when you're not busy playing in the dirt."

What a dick. Parker's hand twitched as he felt his fists clench. "Funny. That doesn't sound like an apology."

Sophie scooted down the stairs. "Look, Nate, will you just leave. Please. Seriously, this is between our lawyers now. Sign the papers, don't sign the papers—just go."

"I'm not going anywhere until we settle this and I'm sure as hell not taking orders from your hired help."

"He's not hired help." Sophie shot Parker an apologetic look.

Nate glanced back and forth between them, a hideous smile pulling his thin lips to the sides. "You can't be serious. You're fucking the lawn boy? Jesus, Sophie, if you're so hard up for money you have to screw the help to get your bush trimmed, you really oughta wait 'til we get a better offer on that timeshare."

Without another thought Parker lunged at him, landing a punch square on his jaw.

"What the fuck?" Nate raised his hand to his lip, pulling it away to look at the blood. "She's really not worth losing your job over, buddy, and I'm calling your boss on this."

"I'm the boss, asshole. And the boyfriend. And if you don't do as she asked and leave, I'm gonna be the guy who breaks your fucking nose."

Nate narrowed his eyes but backed off as soon as Parker stepped toward him. "Fine. I'm going. But you—" He turned and pointed a finger straight at Sophie. "You can expect a long and ugly fight. Especially now."

Electricity zipped through Parker. He hadn't had a physical confrontation with anyone since high school. And he'd never felt that much anger toward another person.

Nate slammed his car door and peeled out of the driveway.

"I'm so sorry," Sophie said, her eyes wide. "Is your hand okay? Let me see."

"I'm fine." Parker realized his fists were still clenched.

"No, you're not. You're bleeding. Come in the house."

He followed her up the stairs, his hand protectively at the small of her back, his body still humming with adrenaline. "I can't believe you married that guy."

"That makes two of us. Come here." Sophie turned on the faucet and held her hand out. "We need to get that cleaned off."

Parker held his hand under the cool water, letting Sophie clean off the cuts. "What was he talking about anyway?"

"You need to ice this," she said, examining his fingers. "Sit." She pointed to one of the barstools at the center island, and Parker perched on top of it. He flexed his hand, noticing that his knuckles were already swelling.

Sophie ran water on a dishtowel then wrung it out and filled it with ice. She placed it on his knuckles, tucking the ends into his palm. "Hold that there for a bit."

"You're really bossy when you wanna be, you know that?"

"Sorry. I can't believe you had to see all that." She looked down.

"Hey. You've got nothing to apologize for. Talk to me, though. What timeshare? What's he giving you a hard time about?"

Sophie took a deep breath and sat on the barstool next to his. "We bought a timeshare together, a few years ago, when we got engaged. It seemed like a good idea at the time. The price was down when we got divorced, so as part of the settlement our lawyers agreed we'd keep it as a joint property until we could get a better deal on it. I was stupid to agree to that."

"And now you need the money?"

"That place on Spruce Street, the one I told you about the other week? I looked at it again, and it's the perfect spot. My lease is up next month. If I had the money from the timeshare, I could totally afford it. Without it, I can't."

"How much do you need? Most of my dad's estate is still in probate, but I've got some money and I can always take cash out of the company. Just say the word."

Sophie shook her head. "No. I'm not taking money from anyone. Joey offered the same thing last week, and I told him no too."

Parker felt his jaw drop. "When did this happen?"

"Last week, when he stopped by that afternoon."

Parker remembered. He'd come home for dinner and had found Joey sitting at the kitchen table drinking a beer while Sophie made quesadillas. He'd said he was in the neighborhood visiting his mom and had stopped by. "Why didn't you tell me?" he asked.

"I didn't think there was anything to tell. I was embarrassed he even knew about it. Nate called while Joey was here, and he overheard us fighting. He offered to buy the timeshare—said he could get the money to me in an hour. I said 'no way'."

Parker knew it was a nice thing for Joey to offer and that the money certainly wouldn't mean anything to someone with his salary, but it irked him to think of Joey trying to swoop in and save the day. Especially without Parker even knowing about it.

"You should have told me."

"I didn't say anything because I didn't want you to offer me money either. I can handle this. I own half the timeshare. I have the money. I just can't access it because he's being a prick. That's what's so frustrating."

"I'm sure. And obviously he's being a total ass. But now that I know, will you let me help?"

Sophie looked down before raising her eyes to meet his. "I'm not good at asking for help."

"I know. But you're not asking—I'm offering."

She sighed. "Thanks. If I can't handle it, I'll let you know. I promise."

"Good." Parker flexed his hand. The ice had significantly reduced that pain, and it was only a little sore.

"Does it hurt?" Sophie lifted the edge of the towel to peek underneath.

"It's fine. It was worth it."

She ran her fingers through his hair. "I don't think anyone's ever stood up for me like that."

Parker shrugged. "I just hit the guy."

"No." Sophie's eyes were dark and serious. "You told him to apologize and you told him to leave. And you hit him."

"True."

"When we were getting divorced, you have no idea how badly I wanted someone, anyone, to stand up to him and tell him to apologize to me and make him leave me alone." Her fingers continued to play with the hair at the nape of Parker's neck.

"What about your dad?" he asked.

She shook her head. "He was too busy worrying about town gossip. He never once told Nate off."

"Now I'm sorry I didn't hit him harder."

"Just as well. He'd probably have sued you. I think you got your point across. And I'm sorry he called you the lawn boy."

"I'm not just *the* lawn boy, I'm *your* lawn boy." He saw the smile tugging at her lips.

Karen Stivali

"Best lawn boy I've ever had."

"Only one you'll ever need," he said, pulling her into a kiss.

The next afternoon Parker left work early and headed straight to the bank. He got a cashier's check, wanting to be able to hand the money to Sophie for the deposit whether she wanted it or not. If she didn't need it, that was fine, but he wanted her to know it was right there if she did.

As he made his way into the parking lot, he saw Chrissie struggling to get a stroller out of the back of her blue Honda Odyssey. One of the stroller's wheels appeared to be caught on something, and she was tugging relentlessly with no success. Part of him wanted to just pretend he hadn't seen her and drive away, but he couldn't do it.

"Need some help?" he asked.

She jumped at the sound of his voice, then sighed when she saw him. "You scared me. I didn't see you coming. Yes, I'd love some help. I can't get the damned thing out of the car."

"Probably because of this." Parker lifted the stroller and untangled the wheel from the mesh divider panel in the back of the van. He freed the wheel and set the stroller down in front of Chrissie.

"Thanks," she said, flipping the latches on the sides so it fell open.

Parker studied her face for a second as she squinted at him in the sunlight. Her brow was furrowed, her expression sad. "You're welcome. I'll see you around."

He started to walk away.

"Wait."

Parker closed his eyes and took a deep breath before turning back. "What's up?"

184

"I've been meaning to call you, you know. Or stop by. I was kind of hoping maybe you'd have gotten in touch after we talked at your dad's memorial."

"Get in touch? About what?"

Chrissie sat down on the rear bumper of her still-open minivan. "About...everything. Parker, I'm...I..."

He could see that she was on the verge of tears again and, as much as he didn't want to be talking to her, he also didn't want to see her cry. And he had no napkins to hand her this time.

"Chrissie, there's nothing left to say. I'm not mad at you, if that's what this is about. Okay? It's over. What happened between us was a lifetime ago. We're different people now. This is your life." He gestured to the stroller and the child he could see sleeping in a car seat in the minivan.

"We're different all right. You're happy and I'm miserable." A tear rolled down her cheek, and she looked away, wiping it quickly on her shoulder.

"Why are you miserable?"

She turned to look at him. "I told you. I made a mistake. You're right." She waved her hand around. "This is my life, every day, all the time. Me and Brice. Don't get me wrong, I love being a mom, but when I pictured myself with kids, I never thought it would be so lonely."

"What do you mean?" He couldn't imagine being lonely with a spouse and child.

She shrugged and fiddled with a strap on the edge of the stroller's hood. "When I was younger and I thought about kids, I always pictured you as the father. And I could see you running around the yard with our kids, teaching them to throw a ball."

Parker's chest clenched. He'd pictured the same thing more times than he cared to remember. "Well, you married Jarrod, so now he can teach your kid to throw a ball. Assuming he knows how."

"I don't know if he does or not. He never spends any time with Brice. Or me."

He wanted to say something cold and obnoxious like "too bad" or "you made your bed..." but all he could manage was "I'm sorry."

Chrissie gave a rueful laugh. "No, *I'm* sorry. I really am."

The church bells rang in the distance and Parker realized it was five o'clock. "Look, I've gotta get going."

"Okay." Chrissie stood up, straightening her shorts. "I've got to run errands and get home. Thanks. For getting the stroller for me."

"No problem. Take care of yourself, Chrissie." He turned and walked away, glad she didn't call him back again. He had nothing left to say.

Chapter Twenty-Three

Sophie looked at the clock for the third time in five minutes. Parker was never late for anything but he'd been due to arrive home an hour ago and he was nowhere in sight. She tried his phone but again it went straight to voicemail. *Stop worrying—he's fine.*

She scolded herself, not just for worrying that maybe something was wrong, but for worrying about who he was with. Ever since the week before, when he'd told her about running into Chrissie and how unhappy she seemed, Sophie had a nagging feeling she couldn't shake. *What if he's still in love with her? What if he wants to rescue her?* She knew Parker. He hated seeing people in distress. *What if...* It was too horrible to think about, yet she couldn't shake the thoughts. *He'd never do that to me. Would he?* She was about to dial again when her phone rang. *Oh, thank God.*

"Hey," she said.

"Hey. Sorry I didn't call."

"That's okay. Where are you? We're gonna be really late." Her stomach turned over as she waited for his reply.

"Yeah, about that." Parker paused. "I can't go."

Oh my God. Her heart pounded its way into her throat.

"What do you mean you can't go? Joey's gonna kill us if we miss his housewarming party."

"I know, I know. There was an accident at one of the job sites today. One of the guys fell off a ladder. He's gonna be fine, but I'm at the hospital with him, and he's definitely gonna need a cast. His folks are out of town, so I'm gonna stay and then drive him home and make sure he's all right."

"Oh no. I'm sorry. One of your college workers?" As sad as she was to hear that someone had been hurt, she couldn't keep relief from sweeping over her. *He's not with Chrissie. And I'm going to hell for being thankful for that instead of worried about the guy who fell off a ladder. Dammit. When did I become this person?*

"Yeah, the newbie."

"Don't worry, I'll call Joey and explain. We'll go see his new place another night."

"That's crazy. You go. I know you're dying to finally see the house. Hell, you should be, you helped him pick out half the damn furniture for the place. Besides, he's counting on you to bring the desserts."

"Shit." She looked at the stack of boxes from Mangiano's. She'd been so worried about Parker she'd almost forgotten.

"Go, you'll have fun. If I get out of the hospital in the next few hours, I'll swing by. If not, you can tell me all about it when you get home."

"Are you sure?" She didn't know anyone else who'd been invited and really wasn't looking forward to going by herself.

"Positive. Have a good time and tell Joey I'm sorry. I'll get there if I can but based on the wait time in this ER I'll tell you right now it doesn't look good."

"Either way I'll see you at your place later, right?"

"Can't wait."

Sophie hung up with a sigh. *Stop being so selfish. And stop being so distrustful. Jesus.*

The drive to Joey's took almost forty-five minutes, but she managed not to get lost. As she pulled up to the house, she drew in a deep breath. She'd seen pictures on his phone, but the photos hadn't done it justice. She'd known Joey had always wanted a nice house. Even as a kid he'd talked about the day he'd be able to afford one. But this wasn't just a house—it was a showpiece. Modern. Tall. All angles and glass. It was an architectural dream.

Sophie rang the doorbell, wondering if she was underdressed. Joey answered wearing a fitted black T-shirt and faded jeans, barefoot. *Not underdressed.*

"Hey." He gave her a broad smile and took the shopping bags from her hands as he pulled her into a hug.

"Sorry I'm late," she said, glancing around. No one else appeared to be there.

"You're not, really. I told everyone else to get here later. I wanted some time to show you and Parker around."

"Well, it's just me."

"I know. He called. Too bad. But I'm glad you're here."

"You're glad dessert's here," she teased.

"You're better than dessert," he said, kissing the side of her head. "Come on, I'll show you around."

Sophie took in the high ceilings and the wall of windows in the enormous great room. "It's beautiful. It looks even more amazing than it did in the pictures."

"Thanks. Wait 'til you get a load of the kitchen."

She followed him through an arched doorway into what was easily the coolest kitchen she'd ever seen. The entire back wall was brick. An enormous center island sat in the middle of the room. It had chairs on one side and open shelving on each end. The eight-burner stove had a grill in the middle, and there were double wall ovens in addition to the two beneath the stovetop.

"Good God, Joey. You could cook for the entire team."

189

Joey grinned at her. "I plan to. And my whole family. Can you see my mother in this kitchen? She'll think she's died and gone to heaven."

"I always loved your mother's cooking."

"Then you're gonna love tonight's meal. She taught me well."

Sophie took in the pots simmering on the stove. "It smells great. What'd you make?"

"I've got lasagna and eggplant parm in the oven, pepperoni bread, extra sauce for dipping and a bunch of antipasto platters in the fridge. And I grilled up a bunch of sausage and peppers. I'm having some other stuff catered in, but I wanted to be in charge of the Italian food."

"To make sure it's right." Sophie laughed when he nodded. She couldn't get over how much he'd cooked. "Geez, Joey. If this whole baseball thing doesn't work out, you should start catering weddings. Not enough good Italian caterers around, if you ask me."

Joey laughed, the sound deep and rich. "You'd hire me, eh?"

"In a heartbeat."

"I wouldn't mind working under you." He gave her a wink that reminded her of flirty high school Joey.

Sophie rolled her eyes. "You need me to help with anything?"

"I was just gonna make a batch of margaritas. I was trying to get this new blender to work when you showed up."

"Is that the one from the late-night infomercials?" She'd seen it advertised but had never seen one in person. It was enormous. And she knew it cost around five hundred bucks.

"Yep. Supposed to be good for everything from soup to ice cream, and I'm sure it will be if I can get the damn thing set up right."

"I don't suppose you read the instructions."

Joey raised an eyebrow. "Why the hell would I do that?"

Sighing, she picked up the manual and started flipping through it. She glanced from the diagram to the machine. "May I?" she asked.

"Be my guest." Joey stepped aside.

Sophie lifted the glass pitcher out of the base, turned it a quarter turn, set it back down and heard it click into place. "*Voila.*"

"Seriously?"

"Try it."

Joey hit the start button and, sure enough, the ingredients started to whir together. "Damn. You've got the magic touch." He lifted the lid off and added ice cubes then reached for a long tamper.

"Don't think you should do that," she said.

"No it's fine, it's not long enough to reach the blades. It just prevents everything from getting jammed up." He reached for another handful of ice.

"That's not what I meant, I think it's too—" Before she could finish talking, he let go of the handful of ice and the blender sent up a large spray of strawberry margarita, splattering the center island and both of them. "Full."

"Shit." Joey slammed his finger on the button, stopping the machine.

Sophie looked down at the red streaks on her shirt, wiping the back of her hand across her wet cheek.

"Sorry," Joey said, his face breaking into a grin as he licked margarita off the side of his mouth. "At least it tastes good."

Sophie laughed and smacked him.

"What? It does." His eyes sparkled with mischief.

He chuckled and reached behind his head, whipping off his wet shirt. Before she could stop herself, her eyes raked over his bare chest. Tan, perfectly sculpted muscles, trail of silky black hair pointing straight down into his low-slung jeans. She looked away as quickly as she could but Joey turned her face toward him.

"Here," he said, wiping her cheek with a dry part of his T-shirt.

His touch was so gentle, so innocent, she held still. When he leaned toward her, she honestly thought he was just taking a closer look. Before she knew what was happening, he pressed his lips to hers. Her brain tried to process what was happening as his mouth moved against hers, his hand cupping the back of her head.

What the fuck? She pulled away, nearly tripping over one of the black-lacquered bar stools behind her.

She stared at him, unable to believe that he'd just kissed her.

His eyes were dark as onyx as he held her gaze. "I should probably apologize but I can't. I've wanted to do that for years."

Sophie found her voice. "What?"

"Come on, Soph. All those years in school. You must have known Parker and I were both into you."

Sophie took another step backward, wondering if she should sit down or leave. "What?" was still all she could manage to say.

"I'm trying to be happy for you guys, but it kills me sometimes, watching you together."

"Have you lost your mind?" Sophie grabbed a kitchen towel off the counter and started wiping at her arms.

"More like I found my nerve. Do you know you're the only girl I've ever had a thing for who I didn't go after? I always told myself it was because we were friends. Truth is I was afraid you'd shoot me down."

She gaped at him. *He can't really be saying this. Joey Nardo could and always had been able to have any woman he wanted.*

"Be honest with me, Soph. Did you ever think about it? About me?"

She felt her cheeks heat. Of course she had. No woman could seriously deny that she'd ever had impure thoughts about Joey. But that didn't matter. "That's not the point."

Joey's eyes lit up and a crazy-handsome smile spread across his lips. "So you have?"

Sophie shook her head. "No. I mean yes, but not now."

He stepped toward her, his fingers grazing her arm. "I can't think of a better time."

"Stop," she said, grateful when his hand froze then pulled away.

His brow furrowed. "We—"

"No." She stopped him before he could say anything else. "We can't anything. Joey I'm in love with Parker. I love him. I can't even think about anyone else. At all."

Joey flinched a little at her words, but he nodded. "You really love him?"

Sophie felt as if her heart might burst. "Totally."

His eyes searched hers and his expression softened. She knew he saw that she was telling the God's-honest truth. He sighed and raked his hand through his thick black hair. "He's a lucky guy."

Lucky wasn't a word she thought of when she thought of Parker. He'd had more hardships than anyone else she'd ever known.

"I'm serious," Joey said. "Women like you don't come along every day. Believe me, I've dated enough to know for sure."

Sophie couldn't help but laugh. "That you have."

"What can I say? You set the bar pretty high."

"I'm trying to be pissed off at you. Stop saying nice shit."

Joey chuckled. "Just being honest. Speaking of which, you're gonna tell him about this, aren't you?"

Oh crap. That was not a conversation she was looking forward to having. "We promised we'd never lie to each other."

"And I suppose that includes lies of omission?"

Joey looked remorseful enough she wanted to tell him no. Instead of smooth, together, suave Joey, he looked like a little boy again. A boy who knew he might be at risk of losing his best friend.

"I'm sorry," she said.

"Hey, I'm the one who's sorry. I should have kept my mouth shut."

Sophie had the urge to throw her arms around him and give him a hug. He clearly knew he'd made a mistake and felt like an ass about it. She hated the thought of coming between him and Parker. She loved them both, she just loved Parker in a completely different way. "I think I better go."

Joey closed his eyes and took a deep breath. "Can't even convince you to stay for some food? My friends will be here any minute. You'll be perfectly safe, I promise. I've reached my quota of stupid moves for the day."

"Maybe the whole week." She smiled. "I really oughta go."

"You want a dry shirt to change into?"

"No, thanks. A little margarita never hurt anyone."

Sophie dialed Parker's cell as soon as she got into the car. *Please pick up.* He answered on the third ring. "Oh good, where are you?"

"Still at the emergency room. He's in x-ray. What's up?"

"I just wanted to tell you I'm heading home."

"Already? What's wrong?"

She closed her eyes. "Nothing, I just decided it wasn't really my scene so I only stayed a little bit." *Not really a lie.*

"Are you all right?"

She could tell Parker knew something was up. "I'm fine. How much longer do you think you'll be tied up at the hospital?"

"Hard to say. At least a few more hours, I imagine. Do you need me to come home now? I can get one of the other guys to drive him if you need me." Now he sounded really worried.

"No, absolutely not. I'm fine. Just come over when you get home, okay? I'll leave the light on."

"You sure you're okay? You sound funny."

"I'm great. I just miss you."

Sophie's mind raced for the entire drive home. *I can't believe he kissed me. Shit. Parker's going to flip out. Do I tell him? I have to tell him. If I don't tell him, I'm lying. And if Joey ever told him and I hadn't said anything, that would be even worse. Shit. Shit. Shit.* She knew he'd be furious with Joey. Would he be mad at her too?

Her stomach turned over with dread. Had she led Joey on? Made him think she wanted him to kiss her? She'd never thought of herself as a seductress. Hell, she'd never even thought Joey ever thought of her that way.

As soon as she got home, she showered, hoping the warm water would help clear her head in addition to removing the evidence of the evening from her body. It didn't work. She pulled on shorts and an oversized T-shirt. Not knowing what else to do, she dialed Cindy's number.

Cindy picked up after the second ring. "What's up, Buttercup? I thought you had your big major league party tonight."

"I did."

"Are you okay? You sound weird."

Sophie groaned. "I'm more than weird. I'm a mess."

"What's wrong?" Cindy's singsong tone turned serious.

Sophie spilled the events of the evening to her trying not to miss any details. Cindy remained so silent Sophie thought the call had dropped. "You still there?"

"Oh, I'm here. I'm just imagining a kiss with Joey Nardo."

"Cin, stop it. I need your advice."

"Sorry. Advice. Right."

"Well?" Sophie tapped a pencil on her desk impatiently. "What do I do?"

"Sophie you know as well as I do that you're going to tell Parker everything. A—you're a terrible liar and—B—the dude's supposed to be his best friend and he just broke the biggest guy-code rule."

Sophie blew out a breath. "I know."

"He has a right to know. And you did the right thing. You were straight with Joey and you got the hell out of there before anything else happened. You get extra points from me for that because, honestly, if Joey Nardo wanted to sleep with me, I'd fuck first, think later."

"Not if you were in love."

Cindy giggled. "You must be really, really in love."

"I am. Shit. I just heard a car door. Parker's here."

"Good luck, sweetie. You can do this. Just be honest and make sure you tell him that you turned him down flat."

"I did."

"I know that, and you know that—just make sure Parker knows it."

Chapter Twenty-Four

Parker was closing the kitchen door behind him when Sophie walked into the room. She loved that they were both at the point where they were comfortable entering each other's homes without knocking. He smiled the second he saw her.

"You okay?" he asked, walking straight over and pushing her hair behind her ear as he leaned in for a kiss.

She nodded and wrapped her arms around his neck, wanting to keep kissing him all night rather than having to tell him about her evening.

Parker smoothed his hands down her back and hooked his thumbs into the waistband of her shorts. "Not that I'm complaining about the welcome, but you sure you're all right?"

Tell him. She opened her mouth but nothing came out. Sighing, she laid her forehead on his chest.

He tensed. "You're starting to freak me out a little. What's wrong? Talk to me."

Sophie slid her hand down his arm and slipped her fingers into his. "Nothing's wrong. Exactly. Please don't freak out. Let's go sit down."

He followed her to the couch. She sat cross-legged, facing him, watching his hand nervously stroke the back of the couch. *You're torturing him.*

"Okay, what's so important that I needed to sit down? Seriously, you're really freaking me out."

"I'm sorry. I went to Joey's tonight." Her mind replayed the evening on fast forward.

Parker picked up her hand and rubbed his thumb back and forth against her palm. "What happened? Did someone there give you a hard time? Because I guarantee Joey would kick the ass of anyone who got you this upset."

"That's not really possible." She took a deep breath and blew it out. "I was the only one there. We were in the kitchen, getting stuff ready for his guests, and the lid blew off the blender and margarita went everywhere...and I think he really only meant to wipe some of it off my face, but he was standing really close and before I knew what was happening he kind of kissed me." The last words left Sophie's lips along with the last bit of air in her body. Try as she might she couldn't force herself to take another breath.

Parker stared at her for a second then shook his head. "Kind of kissed you?"

Sophie tightened her hold on his hand and nodded. "Just for a second. I pulled away, and he said it was a mistake."

Parker stood up and paced across the room, a hand firmly anchored in his hair. "A mistake? What... How do..."

Sophie could see him trying to visualize exactly what had happened and she hated it. How many times had she sat imagining what Nate looked like when he was having his affair?

Her throat burned. "I think he realized he shouldn't have done it as soon as it happened." She wasn't entirely sure that was true but she wanted to say anything to get that look off Parker's face. Hurt mixed with anger. It made her physically ill.

"So typical," Parker muttered. She couldn't tell if he was talking to her or himself. "Good old Joey. Going after whatever he wants. Don't kid yourself, Soph—this wasn't a mistake. He's always wanted you. I knew that since we were kids. But now that you and I are together. Jesus. I'd have thought that would have made a difference. Shows what I know."

"You knew? Because I didn't have a clue." Sophie flopped back against the couch cushion. "I'm such an idiot."

"What? No." Parker sat down next to her. "There's only one idiot in this scenario, and it's Joey. Okay, maybe two idiots, because I didn't see this coming, and that certainly doesn't make me a genius."

"I'm sorry," Sophie said.

Parker's stomach dropped. He searched her eyes. "For what?"

"I don't want to be responsible for you two fighting. I was so happy about how well you were getting along. I love how you guys are together."

His knee bobbed and he couldn't make it stop. "This isn't your doing. I mean...unless... Did you want him to kiss you?"

Sophie's mouth fell open, and she looked him straight in the eyes. "No. Of course not. I love you."

Relief washed over him as he realized she was telling the truth. *Thank God.* Goose bumps ran down his arms. He hadn't noticed how tense he'd gotten until his body started to relax. Sophie hadn't wanted this. It was all Joey. "I'm sorry. I had to ask."

"I know you did. But I don't want you to think that for even a second. You and Joey are two of my favorite guys on the planet, but you're the one I want to be with."

The need to kiss her overwhelmed him. He drew her down on the couch, feeling her warmth as she stretched out alongside him. Kissing her, letting her sweet taste fill his senses, he forgot about everything else. All he wanted was Sophie. Now. Always.

Her fingers tugged his shirt out of his pants as he slipped her shorts and panties down her legs. Wiggling her hand between them, she undid his jeans and began pushing them off.

Parker lifted his hips and shoved them down, kicking them off. Sophie curled her fingers around him, stroking as he returned to kissing her.

His fingers slid inside her. It didn't matter how many times he did it, the feel of her—warm, wet, inviting—drove him wild. Curling his fingertips, he felt along the swells and curves, pressing gently, stroking until he heard her gasp. Every sharp intake of breath sent a surge of electricity through him. He loved knowing that he was bringing her pleasure.

Sophie cried out, her breath rasping in his ear. He kissed her neck, feeling her pulse against his lips, waiting until her breathing slowed.

"Make love to me," she whispered. "I need you inside me."

Eager to oblige, he slid on top of her, but as he braced his right arm against the sofa for leverage a sharp pain shot through his shoulder. He forced himself back against the couch so his weight wouldn't fall on top of her.

"Fuck." The stabbing sensation turned to a deep ache as he tried to move again.

"Are you okay?" Sophie's eyes were dark with worry.

"Shit." His eyelids slammed shut as he tried to will himself to ignore the pain. He knew he'd pulled something when he'd punched Nate, and tonight when he'd been helping Tyler in and out of the car he'd felt it give again. Paired with the tension from the evening, it was no wonder he was having spasms.

He could hear Tanya's voice in his head. "Stress makes it all worse." He didn't give a shit what the cause was. All he cared about was that at the moment he didn't even have the strength to hold up his own body weight. *Jesus Christ.*

"I'm sorry. I can't." He sat up, feeling humiliated.

"Is it your shoulder?" Sophie asked, tucking her legs under her.

"Yeah." He tried to massage the knot out, but it was no use. It spasmed again so hard he cringed.

Sophie leaned forward and kissed his cheek, her warm hand moving his out of the way as her fingers smoothed over his shoulder. "Let me do it."

As she continued to massage, she kissed him. Slowly, then with more intensity. She shifted, swinging a leg across his lap so she sat straddling him. Pressing harder against his shoulder, she found the knotted muscles, kneading them as her tongue distracted him, flicking against his lower lip, swirling its way into his mouth.

She rocked her hips against his erection, her wetness coating him. "You don't always have to do all the work, you know."

"I don't consider it work," he said, clutching her ass, drawing her tighter against him.

Sophie undid the buttons of his shirt, pushing the fabric off his shoulders as she kissed her way down his neck, across his chest. Her lips traced over his scars, kissing them. Her warm tongue erased the remaining tension. Reaching between them, she curled her fingers around him, raising up on her knees then slowly sinking down, easing him inside her.

Parker groaned. Her body was always the perfect fit with his, but from this angle, she felt even tighter than usual. He pushed her shirt over her breasts, leaning forward to take one nipple in his mouth as his hand pressed into the soft skin of her lower back. Sophie raised and lowered herself, swiveling her hips, grinding herself against him. *So fucking sexy.*

Her hair caressed his face as she kissed him. He tugged her hips down harder, lifting off the couch to thrust into her. Easing one hand between them, he stroked her, feeling her wetness coat his thumb. Sophie's breath rushed against his neck in short, hot bursts as she braced her arm against the back of the couch.

Her internal muscles clenched around him so tightly that for a second neither of them could move. Frozen in that instant, he felt as if his entire body might burst. Everything felt taut—his chest, his throat, his stomach. His balls drew up tight against his body, aching for release. As Sophie contracted around him, he reached the point of no return. Clutching her to him, he called out as he pulsated inside her.

When they'd both caught their breath, Sophie eased off his lap. "I'll be right back."

He watched as she scooted down the hall toward the bathroom. Parker's brain was still mush but as soon as he started thinking, his first thought was of Joey. He slipped his boxers and jeans back on.

"You want some water?" Sophie asked. He turned to see her reaching into the cupboard for a glass. She still wore just her T-shirt and when she reached, it pulled up high enough to reveal the rounded curves of her beautiful ass.

"Sure." He didn't care about the water. He just wanted to see her get another glass down.

She returned to the couch and curled up next to him, taking a sip of water before setting it on the coffee table. "You okay?" she asked.

"I'm fine. You're amazing." He leaned in and gave her a kiss.

"Do you want to watch a movie?"

"Okay." He placed his glass on the table next to hers and picked up the remote. Sophie curled up with her head on his lap.

Stroking her hair as they watched the television, Parker wondered how the hell he'd managed to get so lucky. Sophie was, without question, the best thing that had ever happened to him and the most important person in his life.

He noticed that her breathing had slowed, her body resting heavier against him. She was sound asleep. Moving as slowly as he could, he eased her off his lap and onto a pillow. He grabbed the throw from the back of the chair and gently covered her. She looked so serene and peaceful. The opposite of how he felt.

It was past midnight, but he knew he wouldn't get any sleep until he'd taken care of things. He scrawled a note on Sophie's kitchen notepad and placed it on the coffee table then quietly sneaked out the back door. He watched from the porch, making sure she hadn't woken up. She remained still. *Good. No sense in her worrying.*

Parker arrived at Joey's address glad to see that there were no other cars there. He'd been fairly certain that he'd have gone ahead and confronted Joey even if there'd still been a dozen people present but he realized it was better that this stay where it belonged, between the two of them.

He rang the doorbell, taking in the outside of the house. With the lights shining up from strategic spots in the perfectly sculpted landscaping, the whole front of the house glowed. All white, angles and windows. The house screamed money. It was the kind of house that could easily have been on the cover of one of Sophie's home-design magazines. She was always scouting for unique or luxurious places to rent for weddings.

This was exactly the kind of house she always chose. *Is this what she wants? I can't give her this.* Joey obviously could. His stomach turned.

Joey answered the door, not looking at all surprised to see him standing there. Parker's spine stiffened the second he saw him.

Joey stepped aside to let him in. Walking past him, Parker took a quick look around. *Holy shit.* His eyes swept over the enormous great room, which was already filled with every gadget imaginable. It looked like an electronics store and a Frontgate catalog had rented the room to display all their latest products. A mix of anger and jealousy percolated, and he turned, ready to tell Joey just what he thought of him.

"Look, man," Joey said. "I'm sorry, I fucked up. You know I've always had a thing for Sophie and, I don't know...she was here, she was right there in front of me and...I wasn't thinking. I just acted. It was a dick move. I was totally out of line. I'm sorry."

An apology was the last thing Parker had expected to hear. He remained, stunned, staring at him.

Joey scrubbed his hand through his hair and rubbed the back of his neck, looking at the ground. "You know she shot me down, right?"

"Yeah, she mentioned that."

"You know she's the only woman who's ever done that?"

Parker bristled. "You're breaking my heart."

"You don't get it, do you?"

"Get what? That you're used to having women fall at your feet? Yeah I get that. I've always gotten that."

Joey snorted. "Not that. All those women? Not one was a real relationship. You know why?"

"Because you're an asshole?"

Joey flinched and Parker felt a twinge of guilt. "Maybe. But the other reason is because I didn't really like any of them. There's not a single woman I've ever dated who I wanted to actually sit and talk to. And then there's Sophie. God. I'd forgotten how much fun she is. I'd forgotten what it felt like to be around her. This whole summer hanging out with the two of you, it all came back."

Parker knew exactly what he meant. The three of them had fallen into their old friendship and it had felt great. And Sophie was the easiest person to talk to that he'd ever known. It wasn't hard to understand why Joey's old feelings had come back. Just like Parker's had.

"Why didn't you say anything to me?"

Joey looked at him like he was an idiot. "I may be an asshole but I have some sense of etiquette. Even I know you don't tell your buddy you're thinking about his girl."

"But you get her alone for ten minutes and you make a move on her? That's okay with your delicate sense of proper etiquette?"

"Look, I said I fucked up. But this wasn't the first time I was alone with her. I didn't try anything any of the other times. I don't know what happened tonight. Seeing her in my house, in the kitchen, just the two of us. I got a flash of what it would be like if we were a couple. And I kissed her. I swear to God I didn't plan to do it. Shit, I thought you were coming with her tonight."

That was true. And he knew they had hung out before without him. He'd had other opportunities and hadn't done anything. Still. It didn't change the facts. Parker paced, trying to decide what he even wanted to say. The farther he walked into the house, the more he found himself looking at all of Joey's crap.

He'd moved in a week ago but it looked like he'd been living there forever. Every wall adorned with pictures, the patio set with furniture, the dining room cabinets filled with china. *It's like a goddamned suite on a luxury cruise ship.*

Joey followed him, looking around with him. "I still can't believe I live here. I wake up and I think to myself, is this me? Is this who I am now? It's fucking surreal."

206

"I'll bet."

"I'm serious. I mean, you grew up in a nice house. I grew up with mismatched dishes sharing a room with two brothers."

"Yeah, it's pretty amazing what a big signing bonus can buy. I remember both of us planning what we'd do when we got them. Well, you got yours and did exactly what you wanted. You've got absolutely everything you and I both wanted." Parker's throat felt tight. *Every goddamned thing.*

"Nope." Joey shook his head. "Not everything. You got Sophie."

"Sophie's not a thing."

"No, she's not. But you tell me. Would you trade her for what I've got?"

Parker scoffed at the question.

"I'm serious, man. Would you?"

Looking into Joey's face, he saw something he hadn't seen in a long time. He looked lost. It seemed impossible. He was literally living the dream they'd shared since they were kids tossing a baseball back and forth in the park. But the question hit home. "Not in a million years."

"That's why I kissed her."

The last thing Parker had wanted was to feel sympathy for Joey but he couldn't help it. He'd spent so much time trying not to be jealous of what Joey had that it hadn't occurred to him that Joey might be jealous too. Parker sat down on Joey's black leather couch. "You're such a fucking dick."

"Pretty sure I admitted that the second you showed up."

"You're a dick because I have every right to hate you right now and I don't."

"Really?"

"I hate you some, just not as much as I want to."

"You do know how much she loves you, right?"

207

Parker's eyes shot up to Joey's.

"'I'm in love with Parker. I can't even think about anyone else.' Believe me those were the last words I wanted to hear from her. I'm remembering them with perfect accuracy."

"You're doing it again."

"Doing what?"

"Making me not totally hate you."

"I really am sorry."

Parker rubbed his eyes. It had to be nearly two a.m. and the entire day seemed to be catching up with him all at once. He looked at Joey, a long, hard look. He'd known him forever. He meant it. He was sorry. "I'm still pissed off."

"As well you should be."

"Shut the fuck up."

"You want a beer or something?" Joey took a step toward the kitchen.

Parker stood. "No, I think I'm gonna get going."

"Okay. Tell Sophie I'm sorry?"

"I think she knows. You just freaked her out."

"Man. That is so not what I wanted to do."

"Well, someone had to ruin your perfect record."

Chapter Twenty-Five

Sophie awoke with a start. It took her a minute to realize she was on the couch then the entire night flooded her mind. Sitting up, she looked around. "Parker?"

She picked up the notepad that sat on the coffee table.

Hope I didn't wake you. Had to go see Joey. Don't worry. I'm fine. He and I just need to have a talk. Stop by if you have time before work tomorrow. If not, I'll call you tomorrow night.

I love you. P

Shit. She glanced at the wall clock. It was nearly four a.m. She walked over to the window and looked at Parker's house. *Thank God. His car's there. He's home.* She scanned the house, noting that all the windows were dark except for a tiny light glowing from the side of the house. She squinted to make sure she was seeing right. The lights were never on in that room. That was his dad's office.

Sophie tugged on her shorts and grabbed a hoodie from the coat rack. She slipped on flip-flops and headed out into the cool night air.

Parker pulled the wheel of packing tape across the top of the box and smoothed it down to make sure it was sealed. He'd been putting off clearing out his dad's office for long enough. When he'd gotten home from Joey's, he felt the need to put some things in the past, starting with the wall of trophies. He'd gotten all but one row of them packed when he heard the back door open and Sophie's soft footsteps coming down the hall.

"Hey," she said, peering into the room. Her hair was loose and messy from sleep, her hoodie falling off one shoulder. He'd never been happier to see her.

"What are you doing up? It's like four in the morning."

"I woke up and you weren't there. I read your note. Are you okay?"

He put his arms around her waist. "I'm better now."

"Seriously. Did you go talk to Joey?"

"I did. I'm glad I did too."

Sophie's brow furrowed. "Did you two work things out?"

"Somewhat. We didn't kill each other. That's a good start, right?"

She frowned.

Parker kissed her downturned lips. "I think we need some time, that's all. Don't worry."

"I can't help it. I'm good at worrying."

"You're an expert. I know. But this is something you don't need to worry about, okay? Joey and I are big boys. We'll work it out eventually. I just want to know if you're all right."

"What do you mean?"

Parker ran his hand along her spine. His heart beat irregularly as he tried to find the words. "I guess what I really mean is, are we okay?"

Sophie stared up at him. "Why wouldn't we be okay?"

He shrugged, continuing to rub her back, trying to soothe himself by focusing on the feel of her beneath his hands. "Joey's a dick for making a move on you while you and I are together, but he's a good guy. And he's got a lot to offer. A lot of things I can't offer you." His voice felt thick, muddy. "I just want to make sure...I mean if you have doubts...if you think maybe..."

Sophie's soft fingers slid over his mouth. "I love you, you big idiot."

He pulled her hand aside. "I know you do but—"

"No buts. Joey's great. And he's got an awesome house and a cool car and will probably earn more money in the next year than I'll earn in the next twenty, and I couldn't care less. I want you. I love you."

Those were the exact words Parker needed to hear. His chest tightened to the point he thought it might burst. "How did I get so lucky?"

Sophie grinned at him. "You're just a great guy. And it doesn't hurt that you're amazing in bed."

Parker laughed. "Is that so?"

"Very much so." She went up on her toes and kissed him, her tongue licking its way into his mouth. Parker relaxed into her sweetness and warmth. As she lowered herself she looked around the room. "What are you doing in here, anyway?"

"Getting rid of some ghosts."

She scanned the empty wall. "You put away all the trophies?"

"Yep."

"Why? You earned those."

"Doesn't matter. They're my past. I want to concentrate on my future." He turned her head, tipping her chin and kissed her, long and hard, until he knew neither of them was thinking about Joey or the trophies or anything else.

Sophie headed home the next morning, feeling totally at peace. Somehow the nightmare of events with Joey had brought her and Parker even closer. She heard her phone ringing as she keyed into her house.

She'd been avoiding her parents' calls for weeks but today she felt like answering.

"Hi, Dad."

"Well, I'm glad to know you're still alive."

Sophie sighed and sat down at the kitchen table. "One of your spies would surely have informed you if I'd died."

"I suppose you think that's funny."

"Not particularly," she said, reaching into the cookie jar and pulling out a chocolate chunk cookie. *Breakfast of champions.* "But it's certainly true. Look, I picked up because I was planning to call you today anyway. There's something I need to tell you."

"What now?"

"Don't say 'what now'. I don't deserve to be spoken to that way. And I'm sick and tired of you and mom acting like I'm some bad girl who needs to be punished. Try to hear me when say this. I. Did. Nothing. Wrong. No, my marriage didn't work out. Yes, the whole town knew about it. Of course I'm sorry it happened that way, but you know what? It happened to me, not to you."

"As a part of this family your actions..."

"My actions are my actions. And my actions didn't cause my husband to have an affair. His actions caused that. And I'm done talking about all of that. What I want you to know before you hear it from someone else is that for the first time in my life I'm actually happy. I'm in love. With Parker. And he makes me happy." Saying it out loud gave her such a burst of strength she felt an actual head rush. It startled her so much she giggled.

"Are you drunk?"

She laughed harder. "No, Dad. I'm not drunk. I'm not a fuck up. I'm not doing anything to disgrace you or mom. I'm just in love. And you can either be happy about that or not. When you decide, you can call and let me know."

Before her father could answer she hung up. She could imagine the stunned look on his face. No one hung up on the great and powerful Mr. Vaughn. He was the one to do the hanging up. *Not today.* Sophie grinned as she made her way down the hall toward the bathroom, her bathroom, in her house. She breathed a sigh of relief as she turned on the shower, already feeling clean and refreshed.

Chapter Twenty-Six

It had been so long since Sophie had been at a bridal event as a guest she'd forgotten how to be at an engagement party without working. She was straightening the rows of favors when a woman she didn't recognize came up behind her.

"You're Sophie, right?" she asked.

"Yes," Sophie took a closer look at her, trying to see if she could place the face.

"It's so nice to meet you. I'm Tanya, Parker's physical therapist. I've heard so much about you."

"Oh my God, I've heard so much about you too. Hi." She held out her hand.

Tanya had a warm, firm handshake but Sophie could tell she was sizing her up. "Have you eaten yet? I'm starving."

"No, I've been too busy trying to make sure everything's going well. Professional hazard. I have a compulsive need to oversee parties."

Tanya's laughter had a warm ring to it. "I know what you mean. See that guy over there, standing with his arm against the door? I have an overwhelming urge to tell him to take a deep breath and drop that shoulder. Bet you anything his neck muscles on that side are tighter than the skirt on his date."

Sophie glanced at the skintight minidress on the girl next to tense-shoulder dude and had to stifle a giggle. "Parker always said you make him laugh. I can see why."

"I love Parker to pieces. He's a great kid. But I don't have to tell you that, do I?"

Tanya eyed her, and Sophie knew she was expecting a serious answer. "No. I know exactly how great he is."

"Good. Then I think you and I are gonna get along just fine. Let's eat."

Sophie and Tanya chatted as they filled their plates with fruit, cheese and cocktail shrimp. She handed Tanya a napkin.

"Thanks. Is Parker coming? I haven't seen him."

"He's on his way. He texted and said he'd gotten stuck in traffic. He should be here...now." Sophie smiled as she saw him entering the room. She watched as he scanned the crowd, his eyes lighting up when he saw her. A flutter passed through her.

Tanya smiled and Sophie knew she'd seen it. Sophie's cheeks heated.

"Ladies," Parker said, giving Sophie a kiss on the cheek. "Judging by the smirks on your faces, I'm gonna say you two have already met."

"Been talking about you the whole time," Tanya teased.

"Pretty much." Sophie giggled at the slightly worried look on his face.

"He's so suspicious all the time. Have you noticed that?" Tanya asked, popping a grape into her mouth.

"Now that you mention it..."

Parker frowned. "All right, that's enough out of both of you. What's good to eat here? I'm starving."

Tanya gave Sophie a wink. "Go help him find some food. I'm going to go say hi to a friend. It really was a pleasure meeting you."

"Likewise." Sophie picked up a cube of cheese and held it up to Parker's lips.

He opened his mouth, nipping at her finger as he took the cheese. "So, how worried do I need to be about you two gossiping about me?"

Sophie laughed. "Not at all. She's awesome, just like you said."

"Did she give you the third degree?"

"Little bit. But not in a bad way."

"Good."

After Sophie had introduced him to the bride- and groom-to-be and some of her other friends, Parker decided to let her chat and excused himself to go get a drink. He dug around in the enormous barrel of ice looking for a Sam Adams. As he pulled out the bottle he heard Tanya's voice.

"Now I see why you've been in such a good mood this summer."

He grabbed the bottle opener hanging from the string on the side of the barrel and popped off the cap. "I told you she was awesome."

"Yes, you did. I'm still glad I got to check her out myself."

"You're such a mom."

Tanya shrugged and pulled a Corona out of the barrel. She held the bottle while Parker popped the cap for her. "I can't help it. I'm pretty fond of you. And you've been through more than enough. You deserve some happiness."

"I am happy." Parker grinned and Tanya studied him.

"Are you thinking of having a party like this yourself someday soon?"

Parker nearly spit out his beer. *How the hell does she do that?* "Do they teach mind reading in physiology class?"

"No, I'm part gypsy. And I'm right, aren't I?" She leaned closer. "Are you gonna propose to her?"

Lying to Tanya was pointless. "I'm planning to. Just waiting for the right time."

In all the time he'd known her, he'd never seen Tanya get even remotely weepy, but when he looked at her, he saw tears in her eyes. "Aww, kid. Good for you."

"I haven't done it yet."

"No, but you will. I get to come to the wedding, right? I bet she'll plan a hell of a great wedding."

Parker laughed. "If there's a wedding, I promise yours will be the first invitation we send."

Chapter Twenty-Seven

Sunlight streamed through the bedroom window as Parker watched Sophie getting dressed. She looked so beautiful with her hair spilling down across her shoulders as she bent to put on her jeans. All he could think about was pulling her back into bed. He reached around her waist, tugging her off balance so she fell onto the mattress beside him.

He kissed her, groaning when she pulled away. "I really wish you didn't have to go on this trip."

Sophie laughed. "I'll only be gone two days."

"That's two days too many." He kissed her again, feeling her relax as she sank into the soft comforter.

"Mmmmm, I have to go. I'm gonna miss my plane."

"Your plane's not for three hours," he whispered as he nibbled her ear.

"Yes, and I have to go home, shower and get to the airport." She gave him a quick peck on the forehead and hopped off the bed, snatching her shirt off his nightstand.

"Call me when you get there."

"I will." She blew him a kiss and disappeared into the hallway. He listened as she trotted down the stairs and out the back door then he turned to look out the window, watching as she walked across her yard.

He flopped back against the pillows and stared at the ceiling. Two days. It wasn't a long time but he had a feeling it was going to feel like a lifetime. Not only was he going to miss her, but when she returned he was planning to take her back to where they had their first date and propose. He opened the drawer on his bedside table and reached to the back. The small black box fit neatly in the palm of his hand, the velvet so soft it felt warm.

It creaked when he opened it. The shiny diamond seemed to smile up at him. His father had given him the ring when he'd turned eighteen. "This was the ring your grandfather gave to your grandmother, and I gave it to your mom. One day I hope you get to give it to the woman you love."

At the time, Parker had assumed the ring would go to Chrissie. Although they did technically get engaged in college, they'd never made it official. That was supposed to happen the summer after junior year, but by then everything had changed. The ring had remained in its box, in his room, at his house, untouched for all these years. Parker was certain it was time the ring found a new home. On Sophie's hand. *If she'll have it.* He could see himself slipping it onto her finger. Could hear her saying yes.

The doorbell rang, startling him out of his daydream. Knowing that Sophie would have just come in had she forgotten something, he pulled on a pair of sweat pants and grabbed a T-shirt, tugging it on as he trotted downstairs to get the door.

Seeing Chrissie standing on his front porch knocked the wind out of him.

"Can I come in?" she asked, chewing on her lower lip.

Parker remained frozen for a second then stepped aside. "Yeah. Sure. I guess."

Chrissie walked into the house, turning in a slow circle. She wore a short summer dress, flowery, her blonde hair curled, makeup perfect. She looked as if she could have been heading to a party, while Parker stood there, barefoot, one minute out of bed.

"What are you doing here?" he asked, not even bothering to close the front door.

Chrissie pointed to the living room. "Can we sit down?"

Parker raked his hand through his hair, realizing how much it was sticking up as his fingers worked through some tangles. "Okay."

He sat on the end cushion, expecting Chrissie to sit on the far side of the sofa but instead she plunked down next to him, crossing her leg so her foot was practically touching his shin. *What the hell?*

"I would have called first but I was afraid you'd tell me not to come."

Reasonable fear. "I might have."

"Then I'm glad I just came over." She took a deep breath and looked around the room. "God, so many memories in here. Do you remember how many times we made out on this couch, listening to hear if your dad was coming down the stairs?"

Of course I do. "Sure."

"Do you think about it?"

"About what?"

"What it was like when we were together."

Parker shook his head. "No."

"I do." She stood up and walked over to the table by the front window. Running her fingers over the ceramic pitcher, she grinned. "Remember when we knocked this over?"

Parker couldn't help but chuckle. They'd been dry humping on the floor and one of them had bumped the table. The handle had cracked clean off and they'd spent the rest of the night trying out different kinds of glue until it finally reattached. "Krazy Glue and a coat of clear nail polish."

"Did your dad ever find out?"

"If he did, he didn't say anything."

"Those are the kind of nights I remember." She strolled back over to the couch and sat down again, tucking her legs under herself, facing him. Her eyes were filled with sadness. "My marriage is a disaster."

"I told you already, I'm sorry to hear that." He was. For the most part. He didn't want her to be unhappy. But the thought that Mr. Perfect On Paper wasn't so perfect in reality wasn't an unpleasant one.

"I was such an idiot. You were everything I ever wanted. It was so hard when you were traveling. All those away games. I kept thinking that was what it would be like if we were married. That you'd be traveling all the time, and I'd spend half my days missing you. Jarrod was going to be a lawyer. I figured, great, they don't travel. I thought I was saving myself from being lonely. Boy, was I wrong."

Parker stared at her, wondering if he was having some weird dream because what she was saying sounded far too surreal. "I don't know what to say."

"Say you still wonder what it would be like. I mean, don't you ever? We were so good together. Don't you remember the heat?"

"Chrissie that was all a million years ago." Parker shifted, feeling uncomfortable with where the conversation was heading. He'd spent years wondering what it would have been like to have sex with Chrissie. But that was a long time ago.

"It doesn't feel like that long to me. I felt it as soon as I saw you again. Didn't you?"

Did I? Not really. Sure, there was history and she was still an attractive woman, but heat? "No."

"Well, I did. And I can't stop thinking about it. About you." She looked into his eyes and for a split second he saw the old Chrissie. The spark was back in her eyes. He flashed back to their times on that very couch. "It's not too late, you know. We could still find out. We could..." She looked down at her lap then up at him.

"What are you talking—"

Before he could finish his sentence her lips were on his. Her mouth was hot, aggressive, her tongue pushing its way into her mouth. Floored, he sat still for a second then grabbed her shoulders to push her away. Instead of moving back, she swung herself onto his lap, straddling him, sinking her hands into his hair.

He wrenched his mouth away from hers. "What the hell?"

Looking past Chrissie his heart fell into his stomach. Sophie stood in the front doorway, mouth gaping open. "I'm sorry," she stammered, stepping backward, nearly tripping over the entryway. "I left my watch upstairs. I...never mind."

Watching her turn and run out the door, Parker felt as if his head might explode. "Fuck."

He scrambled off the couch and ran after Sophie, catching her just as she got to her car.

"Soph, it's not what it looked like."

"It looked like you were sitting on the couch kissing Chrissie."

Okay, so it is what it looked like. Fuck. "That's not what I meant."

"Jesus, Parker, you could have at least waited until I was out of town. Your bed's still warm from us."

The horrified look on her face made Parker feel like throwing up. "She just showed up. I had no idea she was coming over."

"Whatever. Better I found out now than—" Her voice caught, and he could tell she was fighting off tears.

"There's nothing going on. I swear to you."

"I know what I saw." She scrambled inside her car and yanked the door shut.

"Sophie, stop. Don't leave like this."

Through the window he could see tears streaming down her face. She grabbed the gearshift, threw the car into reverse and pulled out of the driveway at warp speed. Watching her take off down the street, all Parker could remember was the night of his accident. Driving. Upset. Distracted. *Oh God.*

He raced into the house and grabbed his keys off the hall table and jammed his feet into a pair of sneakers. "Lock up when you leave," he yelled to Chrissie.

"I'll wait here. Or I'll come back..."

Parker stared at her for a second. "You don't get it, do you? This isn't going to happen. We're over, Chrissie. We've been over for a long time. It took me a long time to get over what you did, but I did. And I'm happy now. With Sophie. I love her. And you don't get to ruin my life a second time. Lock up when you leave. Or don't. I don't care. Just don't be here anymore. And don't come back."

Speeding off after Sophie, Parker found it impossible to keep the bad thoughts at bay. He kept seeing the look on her face. So hurt. So shocked. Bewildered. And all for nothing. The kiss with Chrissie meant nothing to him. *Please let her be okay.* His accident replayed over and over in his mind as he zipped through the streets.

Shit. What airline did she say she was flying? Praying that he remembered correctly, he pulled into short-term parking and ran through the terminal, scanning the check-in lines. *Where is she?* As he spun around he saw her riding the escalator up to the security checkpoint. *Fuck.* If she made it through security before he got to her, he wouldn't be able to get to her.

He took the escalator steps two at a time, catching up to her just before she showed her ticket to the TSA guard.

"Sophie, please, talk to me."

She pulled away from him. "No. I'm gonna miss my flight. I can't believe you followed me here."

"I'll go downstairs and buy a fucking ticket if I have to and follow you all the way to Cleveland if you don't let me explain what happened before you get on that plane."

People were staring. The transit cop by the security entrance eyed them both. Sophie glanced around, her face flushed. "Fine. But just for a minute."

"Thank you." *Thank you.*

He led her to a quiet alcove near the courtesy phone. "I'm sorry. I'm sorry you walked in when you did, but it wasn't what you thought. Chrissie rang the doorbell right after you left. She was acting all weird and talking about the past and she leaned over and kissed me. It lasted for a nanosecond before I pushed her away and you were standing there. That's all that happened."

"That's all? You were on the couch making out with your old fiancée and that's all that happened? Sorry, Parker. Been down this road before. I walked in on Nate and told myself never again."

Parker cursed Chrissie and himself for being such an ass that he didn't see what was happening in time to stop her. "Listen to me. Chrissie means nothing to me. Nothing. I've known that for a long time but today really underscored it. I didn't know you were standing in the doorway. For all I knew, you were already on your way out of town. I didn't even kiss her back. I pushed her off me. I felt nothing."

As he said it, he realized it was true. He'd have thought old feelings would have made him more curious. That old habits would have kicked in and he'd have at least kissed her back. But he didn't. It all felt totally foreign to him. It felt wrong.

Sophie's face remained tense, her brow furrowed, lips tight, eyes dark and angry.

"Do you really not know how I feel about you?" he asked, reaching out, running his hands up and down her arms.

She didn't pull away. *Please let that be a good sign.*

"I thought I did," she said. "Now I don't...I'm not..."

"I want to spend the rest of my life with you."

Her mouth fell open. "Don't..."

"Don't what? Don't tell you how much I love you? Don't tell you that I wake up every day happy to know you're in my life and go to sleep every night thanking God that we found our way back to each other?"

"Parker..."

"Marry me." He hadn't planned to say it. Not like that. Not with security guards eyeing them from five feet away and Sophie holding a carry-on bag and about to get on a plane. He didn't even have the ring.

"What did you say?" She looked so shocked he wondered if it had been a mistake but he'd said it and he meant it.

"I'm asking you to marry me."

The loudspeaker announced the boarding call for Sophie's flight. *Shit. Answer me. Please say yes.*

"This is crazy, Parker. You can't just propose to me and expect everything to be okay. I just saw you kissing Chrissie."

"And the other week you came home and told me you kissed Joey. You told me nothing else happened, and I took you at your word. Can't you do the same for me?"

Sophie flinched. "That's different."

"How is it different? Apparently we both have people from our pasts who wish they'd paid more attention to us when they had the chance. That's their loss. And their problem. Not ours. You and I are the smart ones."

"I don't feel very smart right now."

Parker swept her hair behind her ear, rubbing his thumb against her cheek. "We're goddamned geniuses. We figured out we're good together. Really, really good together. I expect everything to be better than okay for us. I expect us to have a long, happy life together. Just say yes."

Parker held his breath. He could see it in her eyes that she was coming around, that she wanted to say yes. *Come on, baby. Trust me. Trust us.*

She shook her head. "I can't think straight. And I'm really going to miss my plane."

As much as he wanted an answer he didn't want to push too hard. "Okay. Go ahead. Get on the plane. Have a safe trip. And know that when you get home I'm going to be waiting for you."

Sophie's eyes remained wide. "Okay."

"I love you."

She nodded, but didn't say it back. His stomach clenched tight as a fist. *Shit.*

He watched as she went through the scanner and put her shoes and jacket back on. She turned and gave him a brief wave then disappeared into the sea of people as she headed for her gate. *Two days. She's got two days to think this over and I've got two days to make sure that when she gets back she knows exactly how I feel about her.*

Chapter Twenty-Eight

Sophie drove home exhausted from her trip. The weekend had been nonstop bridal events. Rehearsal dinner, bridesmaid luncheon, wedding, send-off brunch. She'd barely had time to change clothes and brush her teeth. The few phone calls she'd had with Parker were brief, and she knew she'd made them awkward by ignoring the fact that he'd proposed to her in the airport.

He didn't mean it. He panicked. She was sure of it. They had managed to talk enough that she felt confident that nothing was going on with him and Chrissie. Once she'd had time to think more clearly, she'd realized he was right. He'd trusted her with the Joey situation. She owed him the same.

Realizing that she actually did trust him came as quite a surprise. It wasn't that she hadn't thought him to be trustworthy, she just honestly hadn't thought that she'd ever have that kind of faith in anyone ever again. Not after what Nate had put her through. The fact that she felt safe with Parker meant more to her than she could possibly tell him. She only hoped that too much hadn't happened between them. So many doubts. So much turmoil. What if he decided it wasn't worth all this drama? She regretted giving him such a hard time.

She pulled into her driveway, noticing how purple the sky was as the sun made its way behind the treetops. A perfect late-summer night. As she headed up her front walk she saw a trail of flower petals leading from her slate walkway around the side of the house.

She followed them, her heart beating faster. The path stopped at the gate to the backyard. As she opened it her breath caught in her throat. The yard had been transformed. Rose bushes, hydrangeas, a white wooden trellis covered in flowering vines. Twinkling white lights adorned the branches of half a dozen trees that now lined the fence behind the pool. It was exactly how she'd described her dream backyard to Parker. Down to the last detail. She'd told him if she ever got married again she wanted it to be at home, a small group of friends and all her favorite things.

Parker stepped out from under the porch awning and walked toward her, eyes locked on hers. "Did I get it right?" he asked.

Not trusting her voice, Sophie nodded. "It's perfect," she managed to whisper.

"Good. You deserve perfection. You deserve everything you want, Sophie, and that's what I want to give you. Everything. All of me. I wasn't sure I'd ever be able to offer that to anyone. I thought I was too broken. That between Chrissie and the accident I had nothing left to give. But you made me realize that's not true. Chrissie's like the baseball trophies. She's what I used to want. She's my past. All of that is nothing but the past. You're my future. My whole future."

Sophie's heart beat a fierce rhythm in her ears. Her eyes welled with tears. "Are you sure?"

He reached out and tucked her hair behind her ear then slid his hand down her arm, dropping to one knee.

Oh my God.

He pulled a small black box out of his pants pocket. He opened it, and she saw the diamond ring sparkling against the dark velvet.

"I've never been more sure of anything in my entire life. I want to grow old with you. I want to have kids with you. I want to move into a house where our kids have friends who live next door and I want us to spy on them as they sneak out to hang out together late at night. I want the entire world to know you're my wife. I want to share everything with you, the good stuff and the bad stuff. I love you, Sophie. In some ways I always have but it's stronger now. I'm stronger now. You make me a better person. You're what I've been waiting for my entire life. Say yes. Marry me."

The look in his eyes, so intense, so sincere, melted her heart. "Yes." The word came out as a breath.

The smile that spread across Parker's face sent tingles through every inch of her body.

"Yes?" he asked.

"Yes," she said. "Yes. Yes. A thousand times yes."

Parker slid the ring onto her finger and stood, pulling her into his arms and kissing her. She breathed him in, wrapping her arms around him as he held her close. His voice was soft as he whispered against her lips. "I'm aiming for way more than a thousand times."

About the Author

Karen Stivali is a prolific writer, compulsive baker and chocoholic with a penchant for books, movies and fictional British men. When she's not writing, she can be found cooking extravagant meals and serving them to family and friends. Prior to deciding to write full-time Karen worked as a hand-drawn animator, a clinical therapist, and held various food-related jobs ranging from waitress to specialty cake maker. Planning elaborate parties and fundraisers takes up what's left of her time and sanity.

Sometimes you have to lose it all to find what you really need.

Then, Again
© *2013 Karen Stivali*

Photographer Kay Turner is dealt a double whammy when she flies home for her grandmother's funeral to find her boyfriend with another woman. Now with two losses to mourn, she retreats to her newly inherited beach house to clear her head.

Everything at the beach is familiar: the sounds of the ocean, the scent of her grandmother's perfume—and the irresistible smile of James Margolis. The man Kay spent her adolescence pining for is every bit as charming as she remembers.

James always thought of Kay as "a nice kid", but he feels something very different for the woman she's become. Especially when he asks if she'd be willing to part with some of her grandmother's recipes for his new restaurant—and they wind up sharing much more than culinary secrets.

But as their relationship deepens, Kay finds herself caught between the demands of her dream career as a travel photographer, and a chance for happiness with the one man she's wanted for a lifetime.

Warning: This foodie romance contains sensual scone baking, a heroine who discovers one bad apple hasn't spoiled her appetite, and a delicious hero you can't help but crave. Blend well, serve hot.

Available now in ebook and print from Samhain Publishing.

It's all about the story...

Romance

HORROR

www.samhainpublishing.com

CPSIA information can be obtained at www.ICGtesting.com
Printed in the USA
LVOW07s1722100715

445789LV00005B/379/P

9 781619 222038